BROKEN BRUTAL *hearts*

EVA CHANCE

Broken Brutal Hearts

A Crooked Paradise novel

First Digital Edition, 2022

Cover design: The Pretty Little Design Co.

Ebook ISBN: 978-1-990338-97-7

Paperback ISBN: 978-1-990338-98-4

ONE

Anthea

As I WATCHED the coroner load my husband's black-bagged body into his van, the last thing I expected was to find myself crying. But when emotion welled up at the base of my throat and in a prickling heat behind my eyes, I let the tears trickle out.

It would look good to the police officer who was just finishing up the rounds he'd made of the house. It'd look like I was grieving. Particularly important when the widow was forty years her husband's junior, and therefore people might be prone to speculation.

He wouldn't be able to tell that the sensation welling up inside me had nothing to do with loss. It was pure, bone-deep relief.

Clyde was gone. After five years of jumping at his every call and submitting myself to his whims, I was free. And after the initial inspection, the police didn't appear to be concerned that there was foul play involved.

I'd chosen my poisons very carefully. Not a single thing the medical examiner would find should point to anything other than a totally natural heart attack. The toxin had merely primed his heart to fail, after all, not outright killed him.

I'd gotten to throw the final trigger right in his face. Bursting into the bathroom where earlier I'd polished the tiles extra slick, yelling at that asshole exactly what I thought of him and how he'd treated me after bottling up all that venom for our entire marriage. Spitting with anger, he'd stormed out of the shower and immediately slipped hard on the floor. The physical exertion combined with the emotional distress had been the final stab to the weakened organ.

To everyone else, it looked like he'd simply stumbled getting out of the shower and the jolt alone had set off the attack. Nothing particularly surprising in a man just past sixty who was at least fifty pounds overweight and who considered the walk from the front door to his chauffeured car a good day's exercise. That was why I'd picked it.

The most important part of making a death look like something other than murder was to go with a story that would make people sigh and nod as if they'd seen it coming from a mile away.

The cop nodded to me with obvious sympathy as he walked by, and I offered a dip of my head in return. Maybe I should have felt victorious as well as relieved. I'd succeeded, hadn't I? But I couldn't dredge up even a flicker of triumph. Mostly I felt exhausted.

Clyde was gone and I was free, but fresh bruises mottled the inside of my arm, just below the pit, where my sleeve covered them. When I shifted my weight, my hip still twinged with a pain that'd never quite healed.

He'd left a mark on me I wasn't sure I'd ever completely shed.

At least I could move forward, onward to better things now. Or things I was choosing for myself, anyway.

"Are you going to be all right here on your own, Mrs. Hoffman?" the cop asked, pausing by his car.

One of my first acts as a free woman was going to be changing my name back to the one that actually belonged to me.

I swiped at my eyes and gave him a wobbly smile intended to look grateful. "I won't be on my own for very long. My brother is on his way."

The cop gave another respectful nod. "Good to have family support at times like these."

I'd have agreed more if it hadn't been family who'd sent me here in the first place.

As I gave the cop a little wave farewell, a black sedan pulled into the drive, leaving room for the coroner's van and the police car to depart. I waited on the front steps as my brother Ezra stepped out.

I'd barely seen him since my marriage—only once, at Dad's funeral a little more than a year ago. At the time, I'd been too busy sorting through all the possibilities that had started spinning in my head to notice just how much gray had come into his dark auburn hair or how many more lines had formed at the corners of his eyes. Or maybe a lot of that had arrived in the past year now that he was fully in charge of the Noble dynasty.

He walked over, his loafers thumping against the

asphalt, and came to a stop at the bottom of the steps. His expression was more somber than I remembered it usually being.

Had he figured out what I'd done? Was he *angry*? He'd argued with Dad about the arrangement the old man had made, bargaining me away to Clyde Hoffman to secure an exclusive business arrangement, but not enough to stop the marriage from happening. And who knew how much he'd been enjoying the fruits of their arrangement since then?

We'd always had a bit of an odd relationship, my brother and me. He was old enough to be *my* father. I was only a year older than his older son, Roland. And as heir to the Noble crime syndicate, he'd shouldered the weight of many more family expectations than I had. But he'd seen me as more than a possession to trade.

"Anthea," he said quietly, in a tone that sounded like an apology, and then, with a brief glint dancing in his eyes, "Back to your old tricks?"

He wasn't an effusive man, but there was admiration in that question. My posture relaxed, and I almost started crying all over again. This time, I held the impulse in.

Ezra respected me because I was made of the same tough stuff every Noble should be. Because I'd learned how to hold my own among the men who controlled so much of my world, honed my own skills to make myself useful among them.

Dad hadn't known about those skills—I didn't think he'd have approved. But I'd revealed my evolving studies to my brother, figuring he'd recognize the value in them. He'd have a reason to speak up for me.

It just hadn't been quite enough to save me from the marriage altogether.

"I don't know what you're talking about," I said evenly, and the corner of Ezra's mouth twitched with a hint of a smile. The last five years had allowed me to practice my poker face to the point of perfection.

"Let's go home," he said, with a rough exhalation. "Do you need to pack?"

"There are a few things I should grab. I'll worry about the rest later. You can come in if you want."

He looked up at the sun beaming from the clear blue sky. Clyde couldn't have died on a prettier spring day.

"I think I'll wait out here," he said.

I pushed open the door and glanced around the front hall, my mind momentarily blanking. Technically, everything in this house was mine now. I didn't want any of it. What I wanted was never to have to see or think about it again.

I forced myself to walk up the stairs to my room—the small sitting room that held my desk and bookcase and a large closet full of clothes. I'd had to sleep with Clyde in the master bedroom, of course.

A rush of urgency swept over me. I grabbed a large hobo-style purse and started shoving the few items I did actually want to keep—the items I'd brought from home in the first place—into it. A few pieces of jewelry that'd belonged to my mother. Three favorite novels. A scarf, a pair of black kitten heels that never pinched my feet, the laptop with its methodically scrubbed history. The two dresses that'd survived Clyde's purges.

I paused and stared at the outfits stuffed into the rest

of the closet. The clothes Clyde had bought for me, that he'd insisted I wear. Low cut on top, high on the bottom, covering as little flesh as possible at all times. Silk and satin and a maid uniform that was way too "dirty" to be used for cleaning.

A different emotion gripped me, fierce and forceful enough to make my jaw clench.

I marched down to the kitchen, found a garbage bag, and strode back to my room. Then I yanked dresses and tops and lingerie off the hangers in savage abandon. I stuffed everything I could into the garbage bag, slung the purse over my shoulder, and hauled the rest of the stash down the stairs.

Ezra raised his eyebrows when I dragged the garbage bag through the doorway. I gave him a tight little smile.

"When we get back to the mansion, I'm burning all of this in the backyard."

My brother let out a low chuckle. "I'll bring you some lighter fluid to get it started."

He helped me toss the garbage bag into the trunk. As I got into the car, the familiar smooth amber scent of the cologne the Noble men favored wrapped around me. Dad had worn it too.

My throat constricted, and I found myself hugging the purse to my chest. Ezra had said we were going "home," but the Noble mansion didn't exactly feel like home anymore. It was where I'd grown up, sure, but it was also where my father had bartered me off within weeks of my eighteenth birthday.

But he was gone too, and there were other familiar faces I'd be looking forward to seeing there.

"How are Roland and Wylder?" I asked as Ezra got in beside me.

My brother had a damn good poker face too. I only noticed the tick of his jaw and the momentary tightening of his hands at the mention of my nephews because I knew him so well—and because being observant had been the key to my survival.

"Roland left," he said brusquely, starting the engine. "Wylder's had to step up. He's… getting there."

I blinked at him, unable to hide my shock. "Left? When? What happened?"

"He decided he didn't want any part of the family anymore," Ezra said. "Took the funds he could get his hands on and vanished, about a year after you got married." He paused. "I forgot you didn't know. You have a lot to catch up on."

I'd noticed Roland's absence at Dad's funeral, but I'd been too distracted to make a thing out of it—and had known better than to pry about Noble business while Clyde was hovering over me. It'd never occurred to me something this extreme had happened.

Ezra's tone told me that he didn't have anything else to say on the specific subject of his elder son. Suddenly the signs of aging made even more sense. How hard had it hit him to lose the son he'd put so much energy into shaping in his image?

A year after my marriage. Roland would have been eighteen. He'd seen the life ahead of him… and run.

I could have done the same, couldn't I? I'd been facing a hell of a lot worse fate than he had. To a lot of people, he'd thrown away an honor. I strained my mind for any memory that might have clued me in to the fact that he'd been fracturing under the pressure, but he'd gotten pretty distant from me in the last few years before Clyde. I'd assumed he was just focused on finding his place in the business. It appeared he'd actually been focused on finding his way *out* of it.

Obviously Ezra and Dad hadn't been able to track him down. I'd assumed there wasn't any point in me running, that it'd only make things worse. But then, I'd only had a few days to prepare between finding out about my marriage and being escorted into the church. I'd had a lot less access to our holdings than Roland would have had.

And maybe some part of me had believed that it'd have been beneath me as a Noble to run away, no matter what I was facing. Dad had managed to drill that much pride into me, whether it was to my benefit or not.

The engine purred as Ezra pulled onto the road and headed toward the highway. He glanced over at me. "You'll be under my authority now. I'll have plenty of work for you, but beyond that, your time will be yours. Nothing like Hoffman is ever going to happen again."

He meant the statement to be reassuring, but I had the impression of a vise tightening around me. I couldn't help noticing that he hadn't asked how I was or whether I was okay. What I might *want* to do with my life from here. He simply assumed he knew best.

He'd never been exactly warm. Dad hadn't let him be. And now, with Roland gone and the greater responsibilities of leadership resting on Ezra's shoulders, he'd hardened even more.

Was I free, or was I simply moving from one cage to another?

TWO

Three months later

Anthea

Sunlight washed over me, the August heat baking me into the lounge chair on the deck outside the bedroom I'd claimed as my own. I felt completely, bonelessly relaxed for about five minutes—and then one of the Noble underlings came around the house and stopped on the lawn at the edge of the deck.

"Ms. Noble," he said. "Ezra wants to speak to you in his office."

I studied the guy, who couldn't have been much older than me, through slitted eyes. A prickle of irritation ran through me that my brother was summoning me via minion instead of making the short walk down to my room himself, but he had appearances to keep up around the house. Familial fondness didn't seem to factor into that.

Nodding to the lackey, I stretched my legs, and smoothed the skirt of my dress as I stood up. It was part of the new wardrobe I'd been collecting for myself, simple styles that covered much more skin than I'd been allowed to under Clyde's rule, a retro style that appealed to the part of me that enjoyed a little glamor.

I didn't look like any of the other women who hung around the Noble mansion, and that was entirely by design. I expected all the men here to remember that I was as far from being a groupie as they were.

As I went to the sliding door to make my way into the house through my bedroom, my irritation at the summons gave way to a twist of apprehension in my gut.

Since returning to the Noble mansion, I'd gotten away with doing not much other than lounging and poring over all the reference materials and scientific reports to my heart's content. There was something to be said for being able to pursue my interest in murderous strategies freely. I'd put my knowledge to use a couple of times, once in offering my opinion on evidence Ezra's men had turned up at a scene of a skirmish and once suggesting possible methods for dealing with a weapons runner who'd become a thorn in my brother's side, but both instances had been brief.

Otherwise, Ezra had given me a long stretch of leisure in which to recover from my truncated marriage. I appreciated it. But I'd known all along that it could only be a brief respite.

The Nobles hadn't gotten where they were in the

criminal underworld by letting valuable resources go unused.

On my way up the staircase, I crossed paths with Wylder, my younger nephew. He shot me a typical cocky grin with a tip of his head that was more teasing than deferential. "Hey, Auntie Anthea."

I resisted the urge to catch him and give his auburn hair a good rumpling the way I might have before I'd been shipped off to Clyde, when he'd really been just a kid. He was seventeen now, and he was the new heir apparent. He might still exude bravado, especially when he had his little crew of friends around him, but I'd noticed the extra weight on his shoulders right away.

His father wouldn't be going easy on him. Ezra's frustration over Roland's betrayal and disappearance was echoing all through this family. I couldn't exactly tell my brother to lighten up on his younger son—that was as likely to make things worse as better—but hopefully I could provide a moderating influence with similar subtlety to my methods of murder.

Ezra had taken over Dad's former office, of course. I'd already met him there several times before. Stepping inside was somehow both reassuring and unnerving.

It was a relief not to see our father sitting behind that broad desk. On the other hand, Ezra had kept so many of the furnishings the same that it was hard not to slip back through my memories to such lovely moments as the one when Dad had informed me of my impending marriage.

My brother was poised behind the desk in Dad's usual position, but at least the gaze he leveled at me wasn't as chilly as what the former man would have aimed at me.

"Thank you for coming right away, Anthea," he said. Dad would definitely never have offered gratitude for what he'd felt were his basic dues.

"It wasn't any problem," I said, and willed myself to relax as I sank into one of the armchairs opposite the desk. "Why did you want to see me? Are *you* dealing with some problem you figured I could help you with? You know I'm always happy to lend a hand where my skills and knowledge will be useful."

Ezra's lips curved with a tight smile that sent my nerves jangling all over again. He leaned forward, resting his elbows on the desk, his eyes intent on me. "That's what I like to hear. I do have a task for you—a much more involved one than I've asked you to take on before. But I can't think of anyone who'd be half as good for it as you."

If he thought the compliment would butter me up and have me chomping at the bit to go to work for him, he didn't know me all that well, but I kept that thought to myself. I folded my hands on my lap.

"Sounds important," I said. "What *does* it involve?"

"Well… Do you remember the Hell Kickers?"

My stomach clenched up. I kept my expression impassive, giving a slight nod. "I'd have to be an amnesiac not to. I spent a couple of weeks at the Rosanos' place in Brooklyn every summer from when I was ten until I was sixteen."

"Yes." Ezra rubbed his jaw. "I always thought Dad was planning on deepening our alliance with them by having you make a connection with one of the sons. Would have been a lot more age-appropriate than that bastard Hoffman. I'm not sure what changed there. Maybe he thought the alliance was as solid as it could be and Hoffman's connections were a more useful acquisition."

"No doubt," I said with a shrug. He couldn't have any idea how many little jabs his words had sent into me.

There might have been times when I'd had similar imaginings myself—well, about "connecting" with one of the brothers who were heirs to the Hell Kickers empire, not about solidifying alliances for Dad. But the summer when I was sixteen, it'd been made *very* clear to me that as far as they were concerned, I'd never reach more than groupie status.

"And it seems he was wrong there," Ezra went on. "We had a deal set to go down with their people a week ago—a large one. Only one of the men I sent made it back, injured and empty-handed, saying their side opened fire on us. When I've reached out, I've been rebuffed, talked to as if I screwed *them* over. They're pretending the skirmish was our fault to justify keeping both the goods and the money."

I frowned. That didn't sound like the Rosanos' usual M.O. The younger generation might have been made of jerks, and the current boss of the Hell Kickers, Marcel Rosano, had quite the wandering eye—he'd married his third wife during the years I used to go out there. But they were usually pretty reliable when it came to their business dealings. That was why Dad had valued the alliance with them in the first place.

"That's strange," I said. "Was there any sign of hostility from them before the deal that went south?"

Ezra shook his head. "Nothing that struck me at the time, though of course looking back some of the men have pointed to things that might have sounded a little more aggressive than usual or what have you. Hindsight, you know. But obviously we can't let them get away with this. Who knows who'd try to screw us over next?"

"So you're going to war with them?" I asked, not seeing how I'd factor into those plans.

Ezra steepled his hands. "No. Marcel himself wasn't directly involved in the deal. The middle brother, Lucan, has taken on oversight of a certain amount of the smuggling side of things. I'm not sure if *he* screwed us over, or one of the other brothers had a hand in it, or if it's someone prominent working right under them, but I think there's a good chance the boss himself didn't mean to cause any bad blood. I'd rather preserve our working arrangement if I can."

"That makes sense." The Hell Kickers were our strongest allies in the New York area. "How do you want me to get involved, then? Do you want me to have a look at the evidence from the ambush?"

"I'd imagine that will come into it," my brother said, "but like I said, this is going to be a more extensive operation than the previous ones. I want you to go out to Brooklyn, get yourself into the Rosanos' home, and figure out exactly who dealt us dirty."

"Oh." I blinked at him, hoping he couldn't pick up on the queasy lurch of my gut. "But—they're not going to welcome me if they're pissed off at the Nobles right now."

Ezra raised his eyebrows. "I assumed that with your quick mind, you could come up with an appropriate excuse to win them over. Obviously we wouldn't want them *knowing* that you're there to investigate. They should assume you're acting independently of me and for solely personal reasons." He made a vague gesture with his hand. "Just widowed three months ago. Difficult marriage before then. Anyone would be a little unstable. You can sell it."

I probably could. The thought of selling it kept the nausea roiling through me, but I couldn't think of a good excuse for refusing him. My reasons for not wanting to go back there were purely personal.

Well, why shouldn't I go back *because* of those reasons? One or more of the Rosano brothers or someone they'd put in charge had betrayed us, just as they'd betrayed me seven years ago. I could slip back into their lives and show them I was a hell of a lot more than an easy piece of tail. Remind them that *all* the Nobles were a force to be reckoned with.

"Ingratiate yourself with them any way you can," Ezra said. "I want you to identify every person who knew about the double-cross or helped carry it out, whatever you need to do to get close to them and have them let down their guards. That won't be a problem, will it?"

As his meaning sunk in, my chest constricted for a totally different reason. He was asking, not ordering, and maybe if I'd said I wasn't ready to go that far yet, he'd have backed off on me and found another way.

But he'd always remember my refusal. It'd be a mark against me, a sign that I hadn't stepped up for the family when he'd needed me. Who knew how the consequences of that failure might echo through his opinion and treatment of *me*?

He was essentially whoring me out just as much as Dad had done with Clyde. But at least there was a time limit on this scheme and no legal binding. I wouldn't be obligated to put up with whatever they threw at me to make sure I didn't threaten the business alliance—after all, the alliance was already fractured. I'd still be in control.

I needed my brother to know that I was stronger than Dad had ever imagined I could be. That I was worthy of being considered—well, he'd never see me as an equal, but as close to that as I could get.

"Not at all," I said smoothly. "I already know them pretty well. It shouldn't take very long for me to ferret out all their dirty secrets."

"Excellent." Ezra smiled again, this time with enough warmth for it to touch his eyes.

I sat up straighter. "And when I do identify all the people who had a hand in screwing us over? You want me to come back and report to you?"

My brother chuckled. "Oh, no. I think you can handle the next steps by yourself too. You're my expert in killings that don't look like murder, aren't you? I want you to dispatch every traitor in the Hell Kickers in your own special way."

THREE

Anthea

As the cab cruised along the last few blocks before we reached the massive corner brownstone where the Rosanos lived, I gave my eyes several harsh rubs of my knuckles. It wasn't hard to give the appearance that you'd recently been crying. I'd forgone makeup and accessories, wearing only a plain dress that was a little wrinkled as if I'd grabbed the closest thing on hand in my hurry to leave. The only luggage I'd brought with me along with my purse was a duffel bag stuffed with a similar apparent lack of care.

Everything was perfectly considered, of course, for the exact effect it'd create. I was walking into the lion's den, and I intended to put on the best show I could to ensure that I walked back out with all my limbs intact. Maybe I'd even get to recover my dignity along the way.

The cab parked outside the house, and I pushed a few twenties into the driver's hand before scrambling out, lugging my duffel with me. It wasn't that heavy, but I also wanted to give the impression of frailty. Nothing threatening to see here. Just a distressed woman seeking sanctuary out of desperation.

I climbed the stone steps out front, as neatly swept as always, and pressed on the doorbell. The knocker, a bronze ornament that looked like an actual lion's face, seemed to snarl at me as I waited for a response.

I used to find the knocker comforting when I was younger. Like it represented the forces that would protect me while I was within these walls. Now it stood for the men who might tear me apart like the beasts they were if I gave them the chance.

I kept my shoulders rounded, my head low. I didn't know the details of all the Rosanos' current security measures, but chances were good they had a security camera monitoring the front step. My act had to be comprehensive. Even when I was in the supposed privacy of a bedroom or bathroom, I wouldn't be able to let down my guard.

It took a full minute. I was about to jab the bell again when the door sighed open. A musclebound man I didn't recognize peered at me from the front hall, his beady eyes narrowed beneath tufts of reddish-blond hair.

"What do you want?" he demanded.

Such a friendly welcome. I couldn't tell whether he had any idea who I was, but it was easiest to assume no.

I dragged in a breath, purposefully shaky. "I need to talk to Marcel Rosano. My—my father was friends with him, before he died. Abram Noble? I used to come here for a couple weeks in the summers... I didn't know where else to go."

The man's skeptical expression didn't shift. Then his head twitched, and I noticed the bud in his ear—a microphone. He was getting orders from someone.

We were definitely under surveillance.

The lackey waved me inside. The second the door had closed behind me, he motioned for me to hold up my arms. I set down my bag and did so, tolerating the shame of being patted down like a criminal. I'd expected as much.

The guy unzipped my bag and pawed through it, but of course I hadn't concealed anything in a way the average or even above average person would notice. With a huff, he closed it again and pushed it toward me with his heel. "All right. I'll bring you to Marcel. No funny business."

"Humor isn't really my forte," I said, deadpan, as if I hadn't understood what he meant. He scowled but managed not to aim his dour expression at me.

Someone had told him I was more important than a gang groupie or maid. Was Marcel Rosano himself on the other end of that earpiece? That would suggest this underling wasn't all that far beneath the man in charge. I'd better keep an eye on him.

He marched me up the curved grand staircase and down the second-floor hall over the same thick, navy runner that'd covered it seven years ago. The route was achingly familiar, mingling nostalgia with regret.

Dad and I had always walked this path to greet Marcel and his sons when he'd drop me off for my summer stay. *A chance to broaden your horizons and get a sense of the scope of our connections*, he'd told me. I did wonder if Ezra was right—if it'd always been about the hope of solidifying the friendship and business alliance with a marriage.

That would make sense. Dad had clearly never seen me as more than a bargaining chip. It'd never occurred to him that I might be of value to the business in any way except by bringing a man on board.

Just for an instant, I wondered what would have happened if I really had run five years ago when he'd announced my impending nuptials. If I'd rushed to this same house under similar pretenses to now, only those pretenses would have been true.

I already knew the answer, though. Marcel *had* been friends with Dad. He'd have sent me back without a second thought. It wasn't as if the Rosano brothers would have spoken up for me either. They'd already gotten everything they wanted from me two years before.

Would they be with him now, waiting to inspect me and see how much worse for wear I'd come out of my marriage? Eager to confirm that they hadn't missed out on anything worthwhile?

My teeth gritted, and I forced my jaw to relax. As much as I might have longed to stab each of the three of them—in the gut, angled to just the right spot so it'd be a slow and painful but inevitable death—I had a job to do here. And there were things more painful than dying.

I should know.

We stopped outside the room Marcel still used as his office. My escort poked his head inside, and a gruff baritone I immediately recognized said, "Just bring her in, Griffin. She's a girl, not an assassin."

Oh, he really didn't know me as well as he thought he did.

The lackey let out a faint huff and prodded me through the doorway, following behind me. As I went to stand in front of the gleaming white desk where the head of the Hell Kickers gang was sitting, Griffin positioned himself next to the older man's chair.

It was only the three of us in the room, a realization that gave me a rush of relief. I could face his sons, but it'd have been harder dealing with everything at once. This way I could focus on the boss while I gave my pitch.

Marcel Rosano looked pretty much as I remembered him—a hard, grim man with a heavy brow. His carefully trimmed hair was still jet-black, not a hint of gray in it. Considering he was in his late fifties by now, I suspected there must have been dye involved, not that he was likely to ever admit as much.

The room looked pretty much the same too, all posh modern furnishings that contrasted sharply with the aged elegance the Noble men preferred. The only thing my gaze snagged on that struck me was the wedding photo hung on the wall over a side table. At first glance, I thought I'd just forgotten the cut of the dress. Then I registered that the bride's hair was golden-blond rather than the ice-blond waves I'd seen before.

So the senior Rosano had gotten himself out of and then into another marriage since I'd last been here. What was this now? His fourth? He did have a type. I couldn't help being glad that my flame-red hair kept me well out of that category.

He liked them young, that was for sure. The woman in

the new photo barely looked over twenty. I'd bet his sons just loved that—having a stepmom who was the same age or maybe even younger than they were. They'd chafed at following Holly's authority back when I was around to observe, and she'd at least had ten years on Darius, the oldest.

I couldn't say I was sorry to see Holly replaced. We'd never clashed, exactly, but there'd always been something a bit… grasping about her that'd rubbed me the wrong way. Like she expected everything to be handed to her rather than putting in the work to earn it.

I wanted to congratulate Marcel and find out the new wifey's name, but it wouldn't work in my favor to show off my observational skills. I settled for giving him a simpering, nervous smile.

"Thank you for seeing me, Mr. Rosano. I know how busy you must be."

Marcel folded his hands together on his desk. "Your father was a good friend, Anthea. My condolences again for his passing. I wouldn't feel right about turning you away without at least hearing what you've got to say. What are you doing here?"

The question should have sounded concerned, but his gaze felt sharp as a hawk's. He was listening carefully, preparing to analyze every word I said.

I rubbed my hand across my mouth as if I were uncomfortable about telling my story. Which I was, but not for the reasons he'd think.

"I don't know if you heard—my husband passed on," I said. Marcel would have seen me with Clyde at Dad's funeral. "A few months ago. I went back to the family home since I didn't want to stay in his old house alone. But… my brother and I haven't always gotten along all that well. And since Dad died and he took over the business, he's gotten even more set in his ways. We argued a few times, and this morning he got so furious with me that he gave me ten minutes to leave and said he'd have me shot if I showed my face again."

I let a tremor creep into my voice with those last words. Ezra had told me that he hadn't met with Marcel in person since the funeral. All business arrangements had been conducted through middlemen. It'd be easy for the Rosano boss to imagine the already strict man he'd known becoming even harsher under the weight of his responsibilities.

"So why did you come *here*?" Griffin asked, as if he was in charge of this interview.

To my surprise, Marcel only raised his hand in a mild rebuke. The guy was definitely pretty high up—high enough that jumping in like that wasn't overstepping his authority by much at all.

Why *was* Griffin here and not any of the Rosano sons?

When Marcel nodded at me, I answered his lackey's question. "Ezra made it clear he wanted me all the way out of Paradise Bend. I've lived there my whole life. Clyde's house is already sold. I always loved those summer visits here. And I figured it was far enough away from Paradise City that Ezra couldn't be upset about it, even if you two do business together. I didn't mean to impose. I just—I don't have much to get by with. He took over my bank accounts and all that financial stuff too."

Marcel hummed to himself. "Are you aware that we've had our own troubles with the Nobles recently?"

I blinked at him. The woman I was pretending to be wouldn't have been privy to any of her brother's business dealings. "What? No, of course not. Why would— The alliance between the Nobles and the Hell Kickers has always been so solid. I wouldn't have come otherwise. I don't know what to say."

Marcel made a dismissive gesture. "You're not the one who needs to say anything. We'll clear the air soon enough. I can't hold your brother's behavior against you, not when you've been harmed by it too."

My mind latched on to his phrasing—the suggestion that *he'd* been harmed by something Ezra had done. That Ezra needed to say something. Had my brother taken some action to provoke the ruined deal and not bothered to mention that part to me?

It seemed unlikely. Ezra had wanted me to go in fully prepared so I could sort the problem out. It wouldn't help him to lie when I'd only find out the truth from the very people he'd sent me to. Chances were Marcel had simply constructed a public fiction that he was the wounded party. No one wanted to do business with a turncoat.

"If there's any way I can help…" I said hesitantly. "I didn't mean to stir up bad blood."

"Not at all, not at all." The older man paused, leaning forward.

Before he could go on, Griffin stirred at his side. He spoke in a low voice. "Are you sure—when we're still sorting through the pieces—"

Marcel patted his arm. "It's fine." He shifted his attention back to me, his gaze piercing. Analytical.

He was considering how useful having me under his roof might be to whatever negotiations he was going to make. Possibly whether I might have inside info he could coax out of me. I was a bargaining chip yet again.

"You can stay for as long as you need to while you get back on your feet," Marcel said. "I'd prefer if you maintained a low profile and kept to yourself for the most part. I don't want there to be too much buzzing about you being here."

I bobbed my head. "I understand. Thank you so much. Just having somewhere to stay and regroup is all I was hoping for."

"Good." He nudged Griffin. "Take her to one of the guestrooms. I'll have to let the boys know who's come back to visit after all this time."

I stepped after Griffin, restraining a grimace. Somehow I didn't think the "boys" were going to be happy about the news.

FOUR

Darius

I BURST into the section of the third floor we used as our private apartment and was relieved to find both of my brothers already in the large sitting room we shared. Lucan was sitting at the table with one of his ever-present books, and Felix lounged on the leather sofa, jabbing at a video game controller. He paused the game as Lucan looked up.

Good. I could let out my frustration all in one go. Because fuck, I had a lot of it.

But as I took a breath, I reined in some of my roiling emotions. I couldn't go storming around having outbursts for the hell of it. I was the oldest of us; I was the heir. I had to act like I was capable of ruling an empire, or not even my brothers would respect me.

Letting my passions getting the better of me had already led to near disaster before.

I couldn't stop my voice from coming out terse. "She's

back. She's *here*. They're setting her up in a fucking guestroom, and Dad can't even say how long she's staying."

Lucan blinked, his attention sharpening behind his dark brown eyes. *He* never had any trouble keeping an even keel. If anything, he was too calm about too many things.

"Who's here?" he said, setting his book aside. "What are you talking about, Darius?"

"The cunt who screwed us while she was screwing us over," I snapped, and caught myself with a chagrinned huff. So much for keeping my temper.

But when it came to Anthea Noble, I was owed a little rage, wasn't I? I'd never gotten to unleash my fury on the girl who'd deserved it back when she'd earned it. And now she'd waltzed back into our home as if the place belonged to her. The balls on that bitch.

Felix sat up straighter, swiping his floppy black hair away from his face. "Anthea's here? Are you serious?"

My youngest brother didn't sound as upset about it as he should have—but then, women were Felix's main vice. If he'd paid as much attention to running the family business as chasing tail, he could have given me a run for my money when it came to taking the top spot.

"Yes," I gritted out. "Dad just informed me. He got some sob story from her about how her brother cast her out of the home and she had nowhere else to go, and he agreed to take her in. It's fucking ridiculous."

Lucan knit his brow. He rubbed his forehead, displacing the light brown strands that had slipped free from his short ponytail. "Why would he do that? After what she did the last time she was here…"

"Maybe he doesn't care," Felix said. I was glad to hear that his tone had turned more somber at the reminder of the shameful revelation we'd had to face seven years ago. "You know what Dad's like with women. He probably figures her dad put her up to it and she had no choice in the matter or some shit like that. Maybe he's looking to get started on wife number five."

I loved my father, but the thought of him setting his hands anywhere on Anthea Noble's body made me want to puke. Oh, hell, no.

"It doesn't matter what she told him to convince him," I said. "Dad and the old Noble boss were friends for ages. He wouldn't have needed a spy when he could have asked whatever he wanted to know. If she was working for anyone's interests other than her own, it'd be that prick of a brother—Ezra. He's shown he doesn't care about screwing us over either."

"At least he didn't fuck us first," Felix said jauntily, but his bright blue eyes had darkened.

"Her brother is another reason Dad might have let her stay," Lucan pointed out in his usual measured way. "He thinks she knows things about Ezra and his plans that we'd want to find out. He figures he can outmaneuver her—or that we can."

"Yes." I prowled through the room, my rage slowly condensing into a concrete plan. "We have to get everything out of her. Every little tidbit she's got in her head about how the Noble family operates. Everything we can use to show them they can't get away with stabbing us in the back."

Lucan reached into the desk drawer and got out one of

his packs of nicotine gum. As far as I knew, the guy had never taken up smoking—he probably figured he was too smart for that—but he said he liked the boost in alertness and concentration he got from the chemical. I guessed it was smarter to ingest it in a way that didn't also require filling your lungs with tobacco and Lord knew what other garbage.

"She might really have been kicked out of the family home," he said. "Ezra isn't sticking to their father's policies. He wouldn't have been expecting her to come back into the fold after her marriage."

I snorted. "You don't think her rich old husband's death was a coincidence, do you? They totally set him up. Take a few years to make the marriage look legit and then off him, getting direct access to all his holdings. She's a goddamn black widow."

Lucan shrugged. "Maybe that was their dad's plan and Ezra isn't so happy about it. Or maybe he feels she's fulfilled her usefulness. Or she got overconfident and started making demands he wasn't willing to entertain."

"It doesn't matter, does it?" Felix asked, his gaze flicking between us. "No matter whether she really wants our help *now*, she turned traitor before. We can't trust her."

"We have to make her pay," I said firmly. "What do you do with a spider? Crush it under your shoe. We're not a bunch of horny teenagers anymore. We know how to handle a woman. We get under her skin, mess with her until she's panting for more, and then break her until she's ready to spill everything." I shot a crooked smile at Felix. "Shouldn't be any trouble for you, should it?"

He grinned back at me. "Oh, no. I'm looking forward to playtime. I'll have her begging for mercy—and a whole lot of other things—in no time flat."

Lucan cleared his throat. "It isn't just playing. Don't get caught up in the fun of it. That's how she blinded *us* the first time around."

Felix shot him a disdainful look. "Do you think I've given a fuck about any of the women I've nailed? I can make her melt without putting in more effort than snapping my fingers. It's you we should be worried about. Do you even remember where the pussy is located?"

Lucan glowered back at him, his mouth flattening. "Just because I don't spend my free time humping every piece of ass in sight doesn't mean I can't handle a little seduction. Especially when it means defending the family."

"Exactly." I folded my arms over my chest. "It's perfectly simple. We humiliate her just as much as she showed us up back then, we make her crave what we'll never give her, we use her and crack her open and then we throw her out with the trash where she belongs. Any argument?"

Both of my brothers shook their heads, matching expressions of determination hardening their faces. A sense of total certainty came over me, steadying me despite my previous fury.

Anthea Noble was going down, and we were just the men to deliver her doom.

FIVE

Anthea

I'D KNOWN it wouldn't be long before I had to face the younger Rosanos. They did still live in the house, after all —in the same third-floor apartment they had before, from what I'd gathered. I could still picture the layout in my head from lazy summer days tucked between them on the sofa watching movies or playing video games, the guys tossing chips into each other's mouths over my head and jostling against me.

I'd even gone into each of their bedrooms at least once, when we were younger and it hadn't seemed like such a private thing. Each was the same size and similarly furnished, off its own wall of the common room, but with a vibe that'd reflected those three very different personalities: Darius's displaying trophies from the sports teams he'd captained, Lucan's strictly neat with a stuffed but perfectly organized bookcase, Felix's an opulently chaotic mess.

But I wasn't anywhere near the third floor when the brothers confronted me. I slipped into the kitchen late in the evening after my arrival, figuring I'd whip up some dinner discreetly. I was just bringing the frying pan to the stove when the door thumped at the other end of the room.

To my chagrin, I startled and dropped the pan on the stovetop with a clatter. When I spun around, I found myself faced with the exact three people I'd least been looking forward to reuniting with.

It was strange, seeing the guys again. Felix had been fifteen, Lucan seventeen, and Darius eighteen the last time I'd been here. They hadn't had all that much more growing up to do, but the men before me definitely felt like *men* in a way the guys I'd thought I'd known hadn't.

And they were even more stunningly handsome than they'd been before, God damn it. No amount of animosity could stop me from noticing that.

Darius had come in last, shoving the door shut behind them, but he was already striding to the front of the pack like the leader he was. He'd always been tall and buff, and even more muscles filled out his brawny frame now beneath the fitted button-up and slacks and highlighted all the most enticing ridges of those assets. He'd cut his dark brown hair even shorter than before, slicked back down with a few stray spikes jutting along his temples. There was a scar on his jaw, a thin pale line like an extra-long smile line, that hadn't been there the last time I'd seen him.

And those light blue eyes had never been as cold as they were now as they stared into mine.

The younger brothers flanked Darius, Lucan on the

left and Felix on the right. Lucan had grown out his lighter brown hair, which I knew from family photos he'd gotten from his mother. The smooth strands were pulled back into a short ponytail. He stood almost as tall as Darius but significantly leaner, like always. The toned forearms that showed beneath the rolled-up sleeves of his dress shirt proved he wasn't any slouch in the muscle department regardless.

His deep brown gaze considered me with a familiar contemplative air. It held none of Darius' overt chill, but there was a stillness to his stance that I didn't recognize at all.

Felix arched his eyebrows at me beneath his typically wayward black hair, which fell at an angle across his forehead. He folded his sinewy arms over his chest, tipping his posture at a jaunty angle, his foot tapping lightly against the floor. He'd always had trouble staying still. Normally his exuberant energy had translated into jokes and pranks. Now, the intensity in his midnight-blue eyes unnerved me. It wasn't so much sly as outright wicked.

I crossed my own arms over the bodice of my day dress, glad that my preferred style covered so much of my skin. Even so, I felt weirdly naked under their combined gazes. Goosebumps rippled over my bare arms and calves.

No. I wasn't letting them intimidate me. *They* were the ones who should feel humiliated after the way they'd treated me. And if they didn't feel that way already, then I'd get them there. I was the wronged party returning to claim vengeance, whether they realized it yet or not.

Better if they didn't, really.

"The firebird finally flies out of the nest—and ends up here," Felix said in a wry tone that had too much of an edge to it to be really playful. A shiver tingled down my back at the old nickname, which apparently he hadn't forgotten—in reference to my red hair and general tininess, at least compared to the three of them. At five foot two, I was a full head shorter than both Darius and Lucan, and my brow only made it up to Felix's chin.

Not intimidated, I reminded myself. I'd survived Dad and Clyde and a hell of a lot more. They had no idea who they were dealing with now.

"It wasn't planned," I said calmly. "I was in a bad situation without many options. Believe me, I had no illusions that I could run to the three of you as my heroes. Thankfully your dad has some chivalry."

"You assumed you could lean on his loyalty to your dad to get your way," Lucan said. His gaze might not have been as icy as Darius's, but his tone was flatly cool.

I turned to the stove as if I wasn't at all concerned about leaving my back vulnerable and turned on the heat under the frying pan. "I didn't assume anything. I *hoped* he'd be willing to give me a roof over my head while I figure out where I'm going from here. Believe me, I've learned not to count on anyone but myself."

Darius's voice rolled out of him with a hint of a growl. "But somehow you didn't predict your asshole brother kicking you out. Not very independent if you're jumping from one man to another. To yet another, if we count your late husband in that line."

I hadn't so much jumped as been tossed, but I didn't

think it'd help my presentation as an independent, capable woman if I brought that up.

I shrugged and cracked open a couple of eggs to scramble them in a bowl. "See it however you like. Your opinion doesn't particularly matter to me."

"It should," he said darkly. "Because this is our house as much as it is our father's, and you're going to play by our rules too. For starters, you should look at your hosts when you're talking to them."

I glanced briefly over my shoulder at him, ignoring his glower. "Or you'll do what?" Then I returned to my cooking, lashing the eggs with a fork since I hadn't been able to find a whisk. The vicious movement bolstered my resolve. "I haven't had dinner yet. I'm hungry. If you want me to look at you, you could grab me the butter from the fridge."

When none of them moved, I went and got the butter myself, along with a hunk of cheese.

"You can't expect us to believe that your brother really threw you out," Lucan said as I dropped a pat of butter into the pan, where it sizzled faintly. "His recently widowed sister who has no place else to go?"

"That shows how well you know—or don't know—my brother," I retorted.

"We know you, Firebird." Felix tsked his tongue. "But don't worry. You play games, and we can play too. It'll be lots of fun. Mostly for us, of course."

That sounded awfully ominous. And what was it supposed to mean? What did they know about me other than I'd been stupid enough to think we were actually friends…

something more than friends… which had no bearing on our current situation. I could understand them suspecting that Ezra had sent me because of the recent conflict between our families, but Felix seemed to be insinuating that there was something suspicious about me in general.

"I'm not looking to play games," I said as I got out a small knife to cut off a few slices of cheese for my scrambled egg sandwich. "I just want to eat some dinner and then get back on my feet. You can all go back to doing whatever you were doing before I showed up." That was, until I dragged them down into the dirt where they belonged.

"I think you're playing one right now," Darius said, his voice low enough to serve as a warning. The next thing I knew, he'd crossed the distance between us and pinned me against the counter, his hands planting on either side of my torso.

The heat of his well-built body washed over me. My fingers curled tighter around the handle of the paring knife. I twisted around, hating that my hip and shoulder had to brush against him while he had me penned in like this—hating that the contact and the crisp, masculine scent of his cologne woke up all kinds of memories I'd rather stayed banished.

"And what are *you* doing?" I asked, gazing up at him steadily, tuning out the stutter of my pulse.

He glared down at me, his expression still cold but his pale eyes—oh, there was definitely more than ice in them now. They burned into me as if they were dancing with white-hot flames. The passion in them, even if it was mostly anger, set amid his brutally gorgeous face sent heat pooling between my thighs.

Fuck. I hadn't been turned on like this—hadn't really been turned on at all—in years. For all I'd serviced Clyde, he'd never bothered to get me off. I should have hooked up with a few Noble lackeys while I had the chance back home, celebrated my freedom and gotten my long-suppressed needs sated.

"I'm reminding you who the boss is," Darius said, as low as before. His breath grazed my face. "Who you need to oblige if you expect to stay here. It won't be like last time. You'll jump when we call. We'll take what we want, when we want it. Our terms, not yours. By the time we're ready, you're going to be begging for it."

I cocked my head, willing down the flush that was creeping beneath my skin. "Begging for what, exactly? I already know what I'd get if I chased after you. No, thank you. Been there, done that."

"Oh, yeah? We're not the boys you toyed with back then." He leaned closer, his head dipping, our faces only inches apart. Every nerve in my body woke up to eager attention despite my internal demands that I stay unaffected. "I'll guarantee you've never had anyone like us. And you won't unless you dance to our tune. I can tell you're already salivating for it. Poor little widow."

Those last mocking words cracked my shell, but it was anger that spilled out. I raised my hand with the knife and held the blade right below his throat, where it'd pierce the skin if he leaned any nearer. "I guarantee I won't be doing any dancing for you. So back off and let me get my dinner."

Felix let out a disbelieving guffaw.

"Anthea," Lucan said, terse and almost chiding, a tone that made me bristle even more.

Darius's lips simply drew back in a smile so fierce it could have flayed a weaker person open. He raised one hand to close his solid fingers around my wrist. He meant to wrench the knife down, away from him, but I shifted my weight at the last second, and the blade nicked the skin just above his collarbone.

"Oops," I said, not at all apologetically.

That might have been a step too far. Darius made a rough sound in his throat and slammed my wrist against the edge of the counter. I kept gripping the knife as if my life depended on it, gritting my teeth against the pain that radiated through my hand. But a weird sort of giddiness rushed through me in the same moment.

I'd gone five years without being able to openly fight. Putting up with whatever Clyde demanded or did to me —because if I pissed him off, then the deal fell apart. While Dad was alive, he'd have done even worse to me after Clyde kicked me back to him.

And after Dad's death… I'd known that Ezra wouldn't mourn the old man's passing, but I hadn't felt I could count on him being okay with me simply leaving the deal in shambles. I'd ensured my way back into his good graces by extricating myself while leaving all business ties intact. I'd kept the money from the personal possessions, and I'd passed all control over Clyde's professional holdings to my brother.

I didn't owe these pricks anything. I was here by their father's grace, not theirs. And if they kicked me out, fuck them. I could investigate just fine from outside these walls if I had to.

With that sense of power surging up inside me, I raised my free hand and trailed my fingers down Darius's —yes, very impressive—chest. His eyes flashed with something more than fury, and his body pushed into my touch just slightly.

Oh, I wasn't the only one affected by our closeness, not by a longshot. He wanted to hear me beg because he was dying to use me all over again.

He'd never met a woman like the one I'd become.

I gave him a coy little smile and brought my hand back to rest on my hip. "Maybe you're the one who'll be dancing. Seems like I've gotten you all hot and bothered already."

He bared his teeth, and for a second I thought he might ram his hips right against me while his mouth crashed into mine. I wasn't sure I *didn't* want him to, which was probably a problem, but at least I'd have the upper hand. He'd be the one whose control had broken.

The eldest Rosano brother kept his head, though, and took the other perfectly acceptable option. He pushed away from me, releasing my wrist.

"Only in your fantasies, Lady Noble," he said, giving his own old nickname for me a savagely mocking lilt. "Enjoy your dinner while you're getting one." Then he stalked out of the kitchen, his brothers falling in behind him.

The second they'd vanished out the doorway, I sagged against the counter. An acrid scent told me the butter had burned in the pan. I muttered a curse and yanked it off the heat, but a heady sense of anticipation was still unfurling inside me.

The Rosano brothers wanted to toy with me? I'd just confirmed that the game could go both ways. They could play with fire all they wanted, but it'd be them getting burnt in the end.

SIX

MARCEL HAD TOLD me to stay out of the way, but I'd learned early on in my marriage how to move through a house without drawing unwanted notice. And pretty much all notice in the Hoffman household had been unwanted.

I wandered through the open rooms on all three floors of the house, taking note of the comings and goings of the Hell Kickers underlings and the staff. Like in the Noble mansion, a few of the members of Marcel's inner circle spent a significant part of their working day in his home, and lackeys were constantly coming and going to report to or consult with the higher-ups.

The shipment the Hell Kickers had stolen had been a lot of pricy merchandise Ezra had been fencing, collected from various operations around the county. Mostly jewelry and small antiques, he'd said—a hundred thousand dollars' worth. He'd never have done a deal that big with an unknown quantity, but he'd trusted Marcel's people.

I didn't catch anyone talking about the Nobles or the stolen shipment during my first full day in the house, so by the late afternoon, I decided I'd better switch tactics to speed things along a little. After my hostile reception from the Rosano brothers, I didn't want to linger here any longer than required to see my mission through.

I caught the attention of a particularly youthful lackey on his way out, motioning him over as I worried at my lower lip with my teeth as if I were nervous. He looked me up and down, giving no sign of whether he recognized me or not, but the fact that I was here in the house and not dressed like I was about to do a striptease must have given him enough confirmation that I held some kind of importance.

"Hey," I said. "Sorry to bother you. It's been a while since I was last here, and I'm not totally up on who's handling what these days… If I wanted to unload a few heirlooms discreetly, is there someone I could talk to about that?"

The young guy, who I doubted was even out of his teens, cocked his head. "For the big stuff, I think it's Mick who's mostly in charge with that, but I haven't seen him around today. He probably wouldn't want to be bothered. You could try Brant. I think he's been part of some of those kinds of deals, smaller scale stuff. I saw him out back." He jabbed his thumb toward the other end of the house.

"Brant," I repeated. "What's he look like, so I make sure I talk to the right guy?"

The lackey chuckled. "I dunno—brown hair, curly… About as tall as I am? Shout his name, and he'll be the one who answers."

He took off, and I headed toward the backyard.

Since this was Brooklyn and not Paradise City, it was a relatively small yard despite the size of the house. No private shooting ranges here. As far as I could tell, it wasn't reserved for any specific kind of business, only discussions that spilled out there when people needed a change of scenery.

Finding Brant was easy enough. There was only one person back there right now, a stocky guy with curly brown hair who was pacing back and forth across the patio stones as he spoke in low tones into his cellphone. I hung back by the door, waiting until he finished the call, positioning myself as meekly as I could.

As soon as he lowered the phone from his ear, I stepped off the narrow deck toward him. "Brant?"

He scowled at me, more sour than imposing. I didn't think he was out of his twenties yet, so not likely someone who had a whole lot of authority. That was better for my purposes anyway. People who were less practiced, less familiar with how much was at stake, made more mistakes.

"What do you want?" he asked tersely.

I folded my arms over my chest as if hugging myself. "We can talk later if you're busy. But one of the other Hell Kickers told me you might be a good person to reach out to if I had a few family heirlooms I wanted to put on the marketplace—without word getting out."

He studied me, and a faint spark of interest lit in his

eyes. "You're Anthea Noble. I heard you'd crashed the party. What, are you looking to sell some of your brother's shit behind his back?"

I guessed even with my keeping a low profile, it wouldn't have taken long for the underlings who spent the most time around the house to catch wind of my arrival. Marcel might not have gossiped, but there were his sons and that Griffin guy and whoever else had seen me arrive. It was hard to stay totally unnoticed when you had hair as flaming red as mine.

I drew my chin up straighter with a dignity I figured he'd expect from a member of the Nobles, even a disgraced one. "It's my 'shit' too. I'm as much a part of the family as he is. And I'm going to need some money. Can you help me or what?"

He shrugged. "Maybe. I haven't handled anything major when it comes to fencing; I just help out with that side of things when I'm called on. But a few pieces, nothing too big, I could figure out a good place to move them. What kind of heirlooms are we talking about?"

I'd brought a few things with me in case I needed them for this kind of bartering, although what I was really looking for was information rather than money. They were part of my inheritance from my late husband, and I didn't give a crap what happened to Clyde's family relics, but no one here would recognize the difference.

"A couple of necklaces," I said, "gold, one with diamonds, the other with sapphires. A pocket watch, and a first edition of James Joyce's *Ulysses*." Which I'd found almost as ponderous as Clyde was when I'd tried to read it ages ago.

Brant hummed to himself. "I'll put out some feelers, see who's looking. The book will probably be the hardest since I'm guessing there are fewer people looking for those, and the collectors tend to talk to each other."

"Whatever you can manage," I said. "I'll be here. And I'm willing to compromise on the price to move them quickly."

"That always helps." He gave me a scrutinizing look that briefly felt more mature than his appearance suggested. I kept up an inane smile of gratitude, willing him not to see anything beyond it.

"I've got Hell Kickers business to take care of too, of course," he went on. "I'll let you know when I have a chance to get around to it."

"Sure, I understand." I waved off the remark while letting my smile tighten as if getting this money really did matter a lot to me. Better that he saw me as a desperate girl than a woman with deeper schemes up her sleeves.

Brant turned away from me, and I inhaled quickly before I lost the one lead I'd gotten. "I heard some guy named Mick also handles a lot of the fencing. If you're too busy, maybe you could point me to him."

Brant's head swiveled to face me, his expression darkening. "*You* don't want to go talking to Mick."

I frowned. "Why not?"

He studied me again in that penetrating way I didn't like. "How much do you know about what went down between the Nobles and the Hell Kickers a couple weeks ago?"

I knit my brow as if I had no idea what he was talking about. "Something went down? Ezra never mentioned that

—but then, it's not like he ever talked about business things with me."

Brant folded his arms over his chest. "Your brother's people turned on ours. Mick was the only one working that deal who made it out alive. You'd better believe he's gunning for the Nobles now, and he won't care how much you did or didn't know about it. So I'd keep out of his way."

I wouldn't have any choice if I didn't find out who I was looking for. "How do I know who he is to steer clear?"

"He's a tall guy, not too bulky, dark hair down to here." Brant gestured to his shoulders. "I don't think there's anyone else who fits all that who'd be coming in and out of the house regularly."

Good. Now I knew who to not-avoid so I could get some more answers. This guy was saying that the Nobles had mowed down every other guy who'd been working the hand-off? More like this Mick had probably mowed them down himself and kept the proceeds, while blaming the Nobles for it. I could see in my mind's eye exactly how that scenario might have played out—and led to the Rosanos being pissed off at Ezra through no fault of my family.

Which meant the last man standing was the key to this whole thing.

"Thank you," I said with a bob of my head. "Really, I appreciate it." More than he knew.

Brant let out a gruff sound and headed inside. I stayed out back for a few minutes longer, soaking in the warmth of the late afternoon sun, and then I went in myself to get on with my own business.

Unfortunately I'd only made it to the base of the stairs when Felix came sauntering down them. I halted in my tracks, but his gaze had already locked on to me. I held myself firm, unwilling to flee even as a predatory smirk curved his lips.

As he approached, he flicked his black hair away from his forehead in a careless gesture. "And what are you up to, Firebird?"

I raised my eyebrows at him. "Who says I'm up to anything? A woman's not allowed to walk down the hall in this place?"

"Not when that woman is you. I think you should have an escort. Otherwise who knows what trouble you could get into." He stepped close, grazing his knuckles down the side of my arm, and a shiver that was far too enjoyable ran over my skin. There'd been no mistaking the suggestiveness of his last remark.

"I think I learned my lesson about trouble around here a long time ago," I said tartly.

The retort had been meant as a reminder of the trouble he and his brothers had given me, but an emotion flashed in Felix's bright eyes that looked more like anger than shame. Like before in the kitchen, it took me aback. What the hell did this guy have to be pissed off at *me* about?

"I don't know," he said in a voice that'd gone both tauter and sultrier, sliding over me like a caress in itself. "Imagine all the things I've learned in the last seven years. Imagine how fun it'd be to have me teach you them."

"That's assuming I haven't already learned them

elsewhere," I replied dryly. "I didn't leave here for a nunnery."

"Had a good time with your decrepit old husband then, did you?"

My jaw clenched at the acidic insinuation in his voice. I wished Clyde had been a lot *more* decrepit than he'd actually been. Maybe then I'd have sported fewer bruises.

Squaring my shoulders, I stepped closer to Felix. I wasn't giving him the power here, not when I had so much of my own to wield.

"Jealous?" I taunted under my breath. "Maybe there are all kinds of things I could teach *you*… if the thought didn't make me want to vomit."

Felix's smirk turned into a baring of his teeth, but a haze of unmistakable lust darkened his eyes. Oh, yes, I did have some power. The brothers might have used me before, but they'd used me because they'd wanted me. I'd been a cherry they'd gobbled up before spitting out the pit.

Never again.

Felix pushed toward me, forcing me to back up until my heel hit the wall behind me. He might not have been especially tall by regular standards, but he could still loom over my petite frame. As he opened his mouth, I kept my body stiffly unyielding—but then the front door swung open just down the hall, voices carrying toward us.

Something flickered across Felix's expression, like irritation sparking into inspiration. Without warning, he grabbed my arm, yanked open a door just beyond my shoulder, and shoved us both past it.

His hand clapped over my mouth, muffling my yelp of

protest. Ripples of thick fabric engulfed me, along with the smell of wool.

We were in a coat closet, full of winter coats that hadn't been used in months. Only a thin sliver of light seeped through the gap between the door and the frame, giving Felix's striking face a hazy quality as he tilted his head. The voices outside got louder—and stopped just a few feet from our hiding spot.

I swatted his hand away from my mouth. "What are you doing?" I hissed.

"You're not supposed to be making public appearances as part of the Rosano household," he said, equally soft. "Or did my dad not make that clear enough?"

"I could have just *walked away*."

"But would you have? I wasn't willing to gamble on it." He paused. "Now we're stuck in here until they move on. So tragic for you."

As he spoke, his fingers slid over my skin again, the tips this time. They traced my arm from my elbow up to the sleeve of my dress and down again, and I swallowed hard against the wash of heat the contact sent through me. It wasn't a *big* closet. He was standing just a couple of inches away from me. One heave of breath would bring our chests crashing together.

"Stop touching me," I said, but it came out in a murmur too faint to be really convincing.

"What? Like this?" A glint caught in his eyes as he teased his fingertips over me, now following the angle of my arm all the way to my wrist, where I'd braced it against my belly. Then they skimmed up, over the curve of my breast above, just missing my nipple—which was already pebbling, thanks to my treacherous fucking body.

"I don't think you really want me to stop," he whispered, like we were in on a secret together. "I think you're dying to find out just how good you can feel with a guy who doesn't have one foot already in the grave." His voice took on a crooning note. "Poor little Firebird, locked away in a cage with no one to look after her."

I couldn't let him control this situation. He wanted to play me, but I could play him right back. I wasn't the only one with hungers here.

"Maybe I'm not the one who's been lonely," I said, letting my hips sway forward. My belly brushed a solid bulge beneath the fly of Felix's pants. "You seem awfully desperate for a piece of tail."

He snorted. "I've got all the tail I could want here. If I was looking to get my dick wet, I've got plenty of places to go. I want to show you how easily *you* can unravel with the right man."

"And that's you, is it?"

"I believe it is."

He raised his hand to cup my breast fully this time, his thumb swiveling over the peak with enough force to send a giddy jolt through me despite the thin padding of my bra. More heat pooled between my legs. If I didn't get a hold of myself soon, I was going to end up soaking right through my panties.

I trailed my hand down his chest in turn, all the way to his straining erection. He hummed in mocking approval and tucked his other hand between my legs. The press of his fingers against my sex shocked a gasp out of me despite my best intentions.

Felix tsked at me and leaned close enough to murmur in my ear. "Better keep quiet, Firebird. We wouldn't want the big bad men out there to find out what you're getting up to."

He stroked me between my legs, still massaging my breast with his other hand. His fingers traced the dampening line of my pussy and flicked up over my clit, making me bite my lip against another gasp. My pulse thundered through my veins.

It *had* been a long time since I'd felt anything like this. Too long. Fuck.

But Felix wasn't trying to get me off. No doubt he was aiming to take me right to the edge and then back off, dangling my orgasm in front of me as bait. They wanted me to beg. They wanted me desperate for *them*.

That wasn't going to happen in any universe in existence.

The knowledge of his probable plan bolstered my resolve. The heady sensations racing through me faded just a little into the background, enough that I could think even as my hips rocked with the rhythm of Felix's admittedly talented hand.

I curled my fingers around his erection through his pants. His breath gave a little hitch that told me all I needed to know.

I gripped him firmly and worked him up and down through the fabric, matching his pace on me. Squeezing here, rolling the heel of my hand over the head there, putting to use all the techniques I'd learned for a speedy rush toward release when I'd wanted nothing more than to be done with my wifely "duties" as soon as humanly possible.

Since I'd had to take care of my husband one way or another, I'd preferred to do it effectively and fast than feebly and forever.

A rough sound escaped Felix's throat. He was jerking against my grasp now with little thrusts I could tell he was trying to restrain.

He hitched the skirt of my dress right up. His thumb darted over my clit, his fingers pressing my panties right up inside me, and I bit back a moan.

If he was going to up the ante, then so could I. I undid his fly with a sharp yank of the zipper and delved right into his boxers. My hand closed around his scorching, velvety shaft.

Felix muffled a word that sounded like a curse behind clenched teeth. He curled his fingers around the edge of my panties, teasing bare flesh now, and a shudder passed through me. He could feel it—he'd know how close I was getting.

"That's right," he said, his breath tingling over my cheek. "That's my good little slut."

Another spike of pleasure quivered through my nerves. I closed my eyes, and one thought blazed into my mind, grounding me. I had to walk away from this first.

I gave his cock a few more skillful strokes of my hand. Precum glazed the tip. Felix bucked into my palm—and I wrenched myself away from him. In a few swift movements, I'd tugged my dress back down, wiped the wetness from my palm on the patterned folds that would hide the damp spot just fine, and pushed the closet door open.

The men who'd clustered just down the hall looked up as I strode toward the staircase. I didn't even glance at them or back over my shoulder at the coat closet that still concealed Felix. He'd have to stay in there for a while longer unless he wanted them to realize what *he'd* been up to in there—and that he hadn't been the one in charge.

My pussy was aching from the lack of release, but I could go take care of that on my own right now. It didn't dampen the surge of triumph racing through me.

Anthea: 1. Rosano brothers: 0. Suck on that, arrogant pricks.

SEVEN

Lucan

I COULD TELL without him saying a word that Felix had gone off with some half-cocked plan. It was just like him. He'd jumped in without thinking things through, and now he was skulking around our rooms with a thundercloud of annoyance hanging over him.

"What happened?" I asked when he'd paced past me for the hundredth or so time that afternoon.

He didn't answer, only let out an inarticulate growl and flopped onto the couch. He snatched the game controller off the coffee table but then just glowered at it.

Darius wasn't in a much better mood. "She wasn't half as nervous as she should have been," he muttered where he was sitting in one of the armchairs, as if we were in the middle of a conversation already. But I didn't need to ask who he was talking about.

He pushed himself to his feet and stalked to the door. "We just have to keep up the pressure. Not give her the chance to get the slightest bit complacent. Or to forget how much we could offer that she's only getting if she gives in."

Felix snorted as if he found that idea amusing and finally switched on the TV. "I'm sure you can handle that all on your own. I'll jump in for a turn later after you're done with her."

Darius frowned at him, looking like he was about to say something about us sticking together. I suspected Felix would hurt our cause more than help it in his current mood, though. I flicked away the email threads I'd been skimming through on my phone and stood up.

"I've got your back. You shake her up, and I'll watch for any slip-ups that could reveal her real purpose here."

Darius grinned at me with a sharpness to his eyes that leached any warmth from his expression. "Excellent. Let's go tear her apart."

It wasn't difficult to find Anthea. We stopped by the guest bedroom where Dad had set her up first, and she answered the rap of Darius's knuckles on the door with a brisk, "Yes?"

Darius simply opened the door, which didn't have a lock even if Anthea would have wanted to use one. Which she probably would after our visit today. That thought niggled at me more than I liked as Darius headed into the room.

He only made it one step. Anthea must have sprung up at the click of the latch, because she was already there to intercept him before he got far enough to take his hand off the knob. She raised her chin, her scarlet hair flaming over her shoulders, her dark gray eyes glinting with annoyance.

"I don't feel like entertaining visitors right now."

Darius hummed. "I don't think it's really up to you when you're *our* guest. We really ought to be entertaining you more. We're failing as hosts. I figured I'd better make up for that oversight."

He shouldered past her, and she had to pull back to avoid behind bowled over. When I stepped inside after my brother, she narrowed her eyes at me.

I gazed calmly back. It was best to focus on her face— and not, say, the sleek curves only partly hidden under the modest '50s style dress she was wearing.

Who was she kidding in that getup? Darius had been right calling her a black widow. Using her feminine appeal to get what she wanted was old hat for Anthea Noble. Too bad for her late husband.

Darius ambled through the room with a casual air, glancing over Anthea's duffel bag set against the wall across from the bed, the blanket loosely tucked over the mattress, her purse on the side table, the view out the small window. I leaned against the dresser, and Anthea stayed next to me, holding the door open. I guessed I couldn't blame her if she didn't want to give Darius total privacy in which to torment her.

"This doesn't feel very much like entertaining," she said, her voice even and dry. "A lot more like spying. What do you think I've got in my luggage that you need to inspect? Should I empty it on the bed for you? Maybe you're looking to steal a pair of panties to desecrate?"

Darius spun around, glowering at her. He'd come here to unsettle her, and she'd already managed to imply that *he* was the one desperate for her attention. I couldn't help admiring how neatly she'd done it, even as my hand clenched at my side.

She hadn't been this formidable an opponent seven years ago. Of course, we hadn't known she'd been an opponent at all. Maybe she had been hiding this much cutting derision behind her pretty smiles and bubbling laugh.

I yanked my mind away from those memories and focused on her reactions as Darius prowled closer. She held her ground, her jaw firm, but I caught the little hitch of her chest against her dress as he grasped the edge of the door and loomed over her, just inches away.

It wasn't only wariness. Her pupils dilated too, her lips parting just the tiniest amount.

He did have an effect on her, as much as she obviously wanted to deny it.

"Is this better?" he drawled, smirking down at her. "The sort of entertainment you're craving?"

"I'm not craving anything about you," Anthea retorted.

"Sure, you are," I said, quietly but clearly. "Anyone can see it. It's no good lying to us. You wouldn't have hooked up with us way back then if you hadn't wanted to, and we were only boys then. Now you're dealing with men. Why wouldn't you want even more?"

I'd thought about it many times since that evening in our rooms when things had spiraled in a direction I didn't think any of us had completely anticipated. Why had she gone for it? She hadn't pushed for information. She'd had nearly free access to our rooms without using seduction as a gambit.

The only answer I'd ever been able to come up with was that in spite of her mission rather than because of it, she hadn't been able to resist. Some part of her *had* craved us, just like Darius had implied.

The knowledge and the flickers of memory shouldn't have stirred my dick the way they did. Neither should the fierce look Anthea shot me, like she was trying to burn me to death with her gaze. But just like that, I was half hard.

Maybe abstaining all these years hadn't been the best strategy. Anthea had messed with my emotions, made it difficult for me to think or see the situation clearly back then, and I'd wanted to avoid a repeat of that experience at all costs. It wasn't as if I'd run into any women who'd particularly tempted me anyway.

I hadn't counted on running into *her* again. Or how much some part of me would still want her. But there really weren't many women like her out there.

Thank God. Or maybe it was a pity. I couldn't quite decide.

"Once was more than enough," she said, turning her attention back to Darius. "For me, anyway. You do seem awfully infatuated. Who knows what I might be able to offer as a woman, after all—if I was remotely inclined to offer it to you?"

She tilted her head to the side in a way she had to know was magnetically coy. Darius's grin didn't budge. He hadn't kept his cock in his pants all these years—he knew how to handle himself better.

It was a good thing I'd come only to watch.

He skimmed his hands down her arms without actually touching her skin, just a fraction of an inch away. Then he teased them back up again. Anthea's stance stiffened a tad, but I didn't need to tell my brother what else I'd noticed.

His voice dropped lower. "I'm not even touching you, and you're already shivering with need." He leaned in, his lips nearly grazing her temple. "Just keep imagining all the things I could do to you that your old fart of a husband never even considered."

"And you can keep imagining that I'll ever welcome your touch."

He made a dismissive sound as he trailed his fingers across her chest, again not quite touching the fabric of her bodice. Then he sank down, the skirt of her dress rippling in his wake. Anthea sucked in a breath.

He gave her a sharp little smile from down on his knees. "And what are you imagining while I'm down here?" He did touch her then, his hands coming to rest on her calf a few inches below her dress's hem.

She smiled back at him, just as tightly. "I'm thinking you're finally figuring out a position of proper deference."

"Oh, really." Without warning, he jerked one of his hands upward between her legs. As he cupped her cunt beneath her dress, a gasp tumbled out of her—and I was fully hard in an instant.

Darius lowered his hand as quickly as he'd raised it, his smile completely a smirk now. "You're drenched. Your pussy doesn't lie, no matter how much your mouth does."

Anthea glared at him. "I was reading a spicy book before you came in. It's got nothing to do with you. On the other hand, how you'd explain the hard-on you're sporting right now—"

Before she'd even finished speaking, she was yanking her leg up, aiming her knee at Darius's nose. He dodged to the side with a rough laugh, and she shoved past him, smacking his head farther aside with her hand. As she spun around by the foot of her bed, no longer pinned against the door, I frowned.

I hadn't really paid attention to her hands when we'd first come in. Her fingers were smudged with something grayish brown. What *had* she actually been up to this afternoon? She hadn't gotten scuffed up from a book.

My gaze darted through the room, scanning as swiftly as I could—and snagged on a few small smudges on the edge of the window frame. Hmm.

That was all I had time to observe. Darius stood up with a cocky chuckle and shook his head at Anthea. "Lie to us all you want, but you can't lie to yourself. Enjoy your 'book.'"

Shaking his head, he motioned for me to follow him out of the room. He walked with more confidence than the last time we'd left her presence, triumph radiating from his stance.

"Did you notice anything else I should know while we were in there?" he asked me as we headed back up to the third floor.

I turned over what I'd seen in my mind. If Darius heard my suspicions, he'd want to charge in guns blazing. I had the feeling unraveling Anthea's plans might require a subtler approach.

"I'm not sure yet," I said. "I'm going to do a little more digging, and then I'll let you know."

"Just don't keep me in the dark if you turn something up, Lucan," he said, clapping a brotherly hand to my shoulder.

———

Several hours later, I found myself in the dark—in the most shadowy section of the street at the far end of the block from the side of our brownstone on the corner. As soon as Anthea had turned in for the night, I'd gotten my car out of the garage and driven off as if I had business to take care of… which I did, but it'd involved looping around the neighboring block and parking here where I had a view of her bedroom window.

What I'd observed didn't mean she was necessarily going to try anything *tonight*. But chances were that she hadn't done anything already—she'd only recently tested her options. And why would she be testing them if she didn't plan on acting on them soon?

If I was wrong, well, then I'd suffer through some fatigue tomorrow and survive.

I popped a piece of nicotine gum into my mouth. A tingle of alertness passed through my nerves alongside the chilly mint flavor. Fiddling with the radio, I found an upbeat pop station that wasn't my usual tastes but should at least stop me from getting too dozy.

Then there was nothing to do but wait. I'd have brought a book to read, but I didn't want the overhead light running down my battery—or drawing attention to me sitting here in the car.

It took about two hours. Around one in the morning, about an hour after the last light on that side of the house had switched off, a figure appeared by Anthea's window. The light from the nearby streetlamp caught on her fiery hair as she wiggled the screen free and then dropped something I could barely make out in the darkness over the ledge.

With an impressively nimble swing of her legs, she was clambering down the side of the house, gripping what must have been a thin, dark rope. Totally bypassing the Hell Kicker guards who'd be hanging out by the front door. Clever bitch.

I dismissed the flicker of admiration and watched her hop the last few feet to the ground. She immediately turned and hurried off in the opposite direction. She'd traded her dress for a black tee and leggings, and everything below her neck blended into the night.

I gave her ten seconds head start and then switched on the car engine. I couldn't follow too closely or she'd realize something was up.

As she crossed the street, I pulled into the road and drove after her. But just as I passed the house, she vanished from view down a laneway between the backs of the houses the next block over.

I swore through my teeth and peered down the laneway as I cruised past it, not wanting to alert her by following her directly down there. I couldn't make out her delicate figure amid the fences and garages anyway. She'd already disappeared in some new direction.

I'd barely started following her, and now I'd lost her.

Just in case I could pick up her trail again, I circled the block a couple of times, but whichever way she'd gone, she'd kept a very low profile. With a sigh, I drove back to our garage.

Fine. I wasn't going to find out where she was sneaking off to by seeing it with my own eyes, so I'd just have to switch to plan B.

EIGHT

Anthea

It felt pretty fitting to examine the scene of the Hell Kickers' betrayal by night. It couldn't have been much earlier than this when the Nobles and the Hell Kickers had agreed to meet up for the exchange.

The desolate parking lot lay behind a couple of run-down warehouses, not the sort of place anyone with good intentions generally ventured. A sour, chalky scent hung in the air. It'd rained since the shootout, but not hard. A few faint bloodstains still marked the pavement.

By my phone's flashlight, I charted out the positions of the vehicles. It seemed most likely that the Nobles had stopped their truck here, where a few pebbles had been crunched under the wheels, and the Hell Kickers would have parked across from them to leave a good gap in the middle.

One of the marks of blood was right in the middle of the space. Another two lay around where I thought the

Nobles had been and one on the Hell Kickers' side. Based on that, we'd obviously suffered more fatalities, but there must have been other bodies that'd fallen without leaving as much of a mess lingering behind. It was hard to draw definite conclusions.

I did take a little satisfaction from the thought that our people had given back what they'd gotten at least a little before they'd gone down.

Most of the casings that'd been left by the guns must have been collected by the police as evidence. I only spotted a couple that'd tumbled over near the side of the warehouses, lost among the tufts of weeds.

I stalked along the buildings and studied the walls and windows. One pane had been shattered—recently, from the lack of grime on the scattered shards. By a bullet in the fray? I made out a couple of definite, fresh bullet marks on the worn brick.

The second one made me pause and frown. Maybe I'd misjudged the positions of the crews. It didn't really make sense that anyone would have been aiming in this direction if they'd been staked out where I'd assume, unless someone's aim had gone ridiculously wide.

I took out a notepad and made a quick sketch of the layout and the locations of the stains and the signs of shots. I could study it more later at my leisure and see what else occurred to me.

There wasn't much else to see. For the sake of thoroughness, I walked over to a large shipping container that was standing way off by the neighboring building. As I reached it, I paused.

There were scuff marks on the pavement around its

base that suggested it'd been moved recently. The rainfall had probably washed away most trace evidence, but there was a greasy smear about the size of a dragged fingerprint on the far side that didn't yet have much in the way of blown grit clinging to it.

Of course, the cops had probably manhandled the container making sure it didn't contain anything related to the crime. No doubt they'd have hauled it back to the station if it would have fit in the evidence locker.

I made a note of its position, the site of the scuff marks, and possible fingerprint all the same. There was no such thing as being *too* thorough. If I'd learned anything in my studies and experiments at putting those studies to practice, it was that you never knew when a seemingly random detail might become the key to victory.

It'd been overcast during the day, and the lingering summer heat had vanished quickly with the darkness. A cool breeze licked over me. I folded my arms over my chest, wishing I'd brought a jacket, and hustled back to the street where civilization still reigned.

I hailed a cab rather than calling an Uber so that I could pay in cash. I wouldn't put it past Marcel Rosano—or various other members of the Hell Kickers—to be tracking my credit cards and any other accounts they could manage to hack into. Anything that connected to the internet could become a liability.

I had the cab drop me off a few blocks from the house and slunk the rest of the way through the stately streets of Carroll Gardens on foot. The thin nylon rope I'd used to rappel down the side of the house was hanging exactly where I'd left it. I watched the streets around the corner brownstone for a few minutes, and when I got an opening with no traffic in sight, I darted across the street and immediately clambered up to my bedroom window.

It was a little slower going up rather than down, but I made it to my open window without provoking any shouts of alarm. I hefted my leg over the ledge, rolled the rest of my body inside, and was just straightening up with a swipe of my hand over my hair when an unexpected voice stopped me in my tracks.

"We do have doors, you know."

I froze in place, my gaze darting to the spot the voice had come from. The room was dark, only hazed faintly from the streetlamps down below, and the figure standing by the door was little more than a silhouette. Still, I recognized the lean frame and even voice well enough to identify him based on nothing else.

I crossed my arms over my chest. "Yes. Like the one for my bedroom. Which you seem to have ignored."

Lucan took a step forward, bringing his pensively handsome face into slightly sharper focus. His dark brown eyes bored into me. "It's my house. Every room is my room if I happen to want to be in it. Where did you go that you wanted to keep such a secret?"

I cocked my head. "Here's the thing about secrets: they stop being a secret if you start telling people about them."

Lucan's expression tensed. I was pissing him off— good. It'd pissed *me* off when he'd just stood there watching while Darius practiced his seductive skills on me this afternoon.

Way back when, I'd always felt a little more connected to the middle Rosano brother than the other two, as much as I'd thought I'd gotten along with all three of them. Lucan understood the appeal of books and absorbing knowledge, like I did. He said what he meant without posturing or sly asides, which had been a relief after all the politicking even within the Noble family back home.

At least, I'd thought he'd said what he meant. He'd clearly been hiding some things from me and lying about others, or we wouldn't have ended up here.

The frustration—no, *anger*—stirred up by that thought propelled me across the room.

"If you're not going to come clean, I can tell my father that you were sneaking around and hiding things that could be dangerous to the family," Lucan said.

I came to a halt just a couple of feet from him, watching the way his chest rose with an abruptly drawn in breath, the way his hands closed at his sides. As if my being this close affected him. As if he were holding himself back from touching me.

I smiled sweetly up at him. "Is that what you've lowered yourself to, Lucan? Are you Daddy's lapdog, running off to him to yap about how the mean lady wouldn't answer your questions?"

"Or I could do whatever it takes to get the answers out of you myself," he retorted.

"And what's that?" I pressed my advantage, seeing his reactions, remembering how I'd gotten Felix off balance. Leaning forward, I slid my hand down his chest. "Maybe I'll enjoy it."

Lucan's voice hardened. "Not as much as I will."

He pushed me backward without warning, crowding me until I reached the edge of the bed. Rather than let him call the shots any farther than that, I took charge in the only direction I was sure I could compel him—grabbing him by his shirt collar and yanking him down with me on the mattress.

He caught himself on his hands, braced over me, his pale eyes flaring in the dimness. Before he could pull away, I tucked my knee between his legs and slid it against the hardness behind his fly. "You *are* enjoying this quite a bit. What a depraved man you've become. But I'm not a kid anymore either. You can't play me the same way you did back then."

"Play *you*?" Lucan sputtered before he clenched his jaw. Instead of jerking away, he dipped closer, his gaze fixed on my face. "This is all a game to you, of course. Except you can't help getting off on it too. Are you as wet now as you were for Darius?"

I fluttered my eyelashes at him. "Are you brave enough to check and find out?"

I hitched my knee a little faster, provoking a tic in Lucan's cheek. He shoved his hand down my leggings to finger my panties, and I bit my lip against a gasp.

For all the roughness of his words and the initial motion, he stroked over the admittedly damp fabric with shocking tenderness. It woke up way too many of my nerves to tingling alertness. As he increased the pressure, I felt more slickness seep out of me.

Lucan smiled, but it was a cold smile, all cruel satisfaction. He rocked his hand against me, studying my reactions with the analytical gaze that missed so little. Heat tickled across my cheeks, but I managed to keep my face impassive, my lips shut.

It shouldn't feel this good, but it did. I wasn't sure how much it was his fingers rubbing up and down over my pussy, his thumb pushing down on my clit with each pulse of his hand, and how much the feel of him hard against my leg, knowing I had *him* heated up too. I could bring him to the brink, and as soon as he made a move for more, I'd leave him with the worst case of blue balls in the history of the universe.

I adjusted the strokes of my leg to make sure I was working him from base to head, brushing his balls each time I lowered my knee. A flush was creeping across his face too, and maybe a faint sheen of sweat at the top of his brow. His hand flicked faster against my sensitive flesh, and I swallowed down a whimper. Pleasure was spreading all through my core along with an urgent need for more, but I couldn't let him see how much he'd affected me.

"I'm going to make you come undone, but not the way you want," he promised, but there was a faint waver in his voice, as if he wasn't as sure of himself as he wanted to sound.

How many women had he been with since me? The caress of his hand against my sex wasn't particularly practiced—and that was part of what was turning me on so quickly. It didn't feel like a man going through the motions but something raw and hungry.

I inhaled as evenly as I could to steady my own voice. I could make use of his unsettled state.

"Whatever you want to believe. I'm not sure you're in control *any* way you think you are. I hear an entire deal with my brother went wrong under your watch? You haven't questioned this Mick guy about how it all fell apart? Too busy trying to prove what a tough guy you are to the ladies, I guess."

"Mick's been through enough," Lucan said with an edge in his voice. "He practically died thanks to your brother's people—or should I say *your* people? He had to watch good men die."

So he really believed that. I guessed that explained some of his hostility toward me, even though I hadn't known anything about the deal until well after it'd gone down, regardless of who was to blame.

I opened my mouth to question him further and immediately shut it again to clamp down on a moan. Heat was surging up from my pussy, the tension building and unfurling at the same time. More than anything, I wanted to clamp my thighs around his hand to urge him on, but the second I showed I was that into his attentions, he'd stop.

I focused as much as I could on the stroke of my leg against his groin. I teased my fingers along the side of his neck to distract him from examining my responses, and his eyes flickered shut. His hand hitched against me, swiveling over my clit at just the right speed, once, twice, with a fresh burst of pleasure—

A dam broke inside me. As I came, I couldn't keep quiet. A choked cry burst from my lips; my head arched back against the bedspread. Pleasure washed all through my body like I hadn't felt in years, not from someone else's touch.

Lucan yanked himself away. He stared down at me, his cock straining against his slacks, his eyes startlingly wild.

"Fuck," he spat at me, and marched out of the room without another word.

I pushed myself upright on shaky arms, watching the door thump shut behind him. My breath rushed in and out of my lungs raggedly. The afterglow of the momentary physical release was already fading.

Technically, I'd won. He'd meant to tease me until I was begging without letting me tip over the edge, but I'd gotten off despite his intentions, while he'd been left hard as a rock. I *should* be triumphant.

So why did I feel like I'd lost something by falling apart at the stroke of his hand?

NINE

Anthea

I slipped from my room the next morning with less confidence than usual. On the outside, I could be as cool and firm as diamond, but I wasn't sure how my insides would react if I ran into Lucan.

Thankfully, I didn't encounter any of the Rosano brothers on my way to the kitchen to scrounge up some breakfast. And my luck held even after. I was just leaving the kitchen when a gruff voice reached my ears from the direction of the front hall.

"Mick! About time you came back around."

I slunk toward the hall quickly enough to make out the answer, though that voice was lower. "The boss has a job for me. I come when called."

Maybe some resentment about his status as a lackey? I hadn't picked up on any sourness in his nonchalant tone, but it was hard to say across this distance.

I eased toward the stairs, checking that no one was observing me. As Mick headed up, I caught a glimpse of him: shoulder-length hair that was black flecked with gray, a frame corded with lean sinewy muscle. He might have been getting on in his years, maybe halfway through his forties, but he didn't look like any kind of weakling.

I dawdled for a few moments near the base of the stairs and then headed up with a distracted air as if I were simply wandering back to my bedroom. Mick would have disappeared in the opposite direction, into Marcel's office.

What excuse did I have to head that way? There was a bathroom nearby. I veered toward it.

Out of view of the stairs, I edged toward the door to the office. No one was in the hall outside. If I heard someone heading this way—from within the room or the other end of the hall—I could dash into the bathroom and pretend I'd been in there the whole time.

The conversation had started while I was making my approach. It sounded like Marcel had already given Mick his marching orders. Mick was responding in a low voice. "I can definitely handle that. Should I be reporting to you or to Lucan?"

"Given the circumstances, I wanted to oversee this deal myself," Marcel said. "I assume you'll exercise more caution this time?"

Mick's tone became terse. "I don't believe there were any signs I could have missed the last time. Believe me, I've spent plenty of hours trying to think of how I could have saved any of those men from the Nobles' bullets."

So he was giving Marcel the same story everyone else

had heard about our people turning on theirs—interesting. It seemed as though none of the Rosanos knew any differently. I'd thought it might be a conspiracy between just them and their trusted underling. What could his endgame be?

"We'll have to approach all our supposed allies with more caution from here on, I suppose," Marcel said with a sigh. "There was once *some* honor among thieves. Well, no good mourning the old days. You're clear on the details?"

"No questions here. Looks pretty standard. I'll handle this without a hitch like I always did before that one disaster. You know I've never let the Hell Kickers down before."

"I do. Let's show we're still just as much in business as we always were."

I recognized the dismissal and darted to the bathroom. I had the door shut before the one to Marcel's office even opened. Marcel strode by with firm strides like a man with a mission.

What was he up to now? Could I use this new job to confirm my suspicions? I had no idea what or where it was, though.

His footsteps faded away—and others rasped past me. There was a knock on the office door, and a brusque voice I recognized as Griffin's. "It's me."

A very casual announcement for an average underling. But this guy hadn't seemed to have an average level of access earlier either. I hesitated as Marcel called him in, and then snuck out to resume my listening.

"…sure Mick can handle it just fine," Marcel was saying.

"It is his specialty, right?" Griffin chuckled. "You pick good people. I think I've gotten together a great team for our next moves."

Next moves for what? My ears pricked.

"Excellent," Marcel said. "I've confirmed the location. Those bastards are going to learn what happens when you try to screw over the Hell Kickers. The place on Orvil Street should make for a perfect start." He paused. "I just wish…"

"You're doing the right thing," Griffin cut in before Marcel could finish his thought. "They haven't given you anything. Cracking down hard, showing your strength— that's why you're the man I always want leading me."

He was laying on the praise thick, but Marcel gave a pleased laugh, clearly eating it up. "And you're proving yourself invaluable. I appreciate how well you've stepped up, Griffin. Maybe you should consult with Darius about—"

Griffin made a scoffing sound. "Oh, I already tried to talk to him about working together. He blew me off, too busy with his gambling rackets, I guess. Seems like that's the only part of the empire *he* cares about."

I frowned. It'd been obvious to me that Darius and his younger brothers were *very* protective of their family legacy. That was half of the reason, maybe the whole reason, they were harassing me. Had Griffin even talked to the oldest Rosano brother, or was he making that up?

What was *his* game here?

But those thoughts were overwhelmed by the spinning in my head as I considered their earlier remarks. Screwing over the Hell Kickers—had someone else done that recently, or had Marcel been talking about the Nobles? What was he planning on doing that he felt would teach *my* family a lesson?

The men in the room didn't seem inclined to fill me in. Griffin started talking about his shitty dad and how glad he was to have gotten out of that house and be really making something of himself, and I heard the floor creak near the top of the stairs. I hustled away before I could get caught eavesdropping. It'd sounded like the most specific parts of the scheme had been discussed previously, and Marcel had simply been setting things in motion.

What was on Orvil Street?

As I stewed over that, I noticed Darius heading down the stairs from his third-floor rooms. His gaze latched on to me. I considered heading to my bedroom, but he'd already shown he was perfectly happy to follow me there. Better to detour to somewhere more public, I suspected.

I walked down the stairs at a brisk but not panicked pace. Down the hall, voices carried from the kitchen. Well, I'd just make myself some tea. That was a perfectly normal thing people did that had nothing to do with fleeing from gang heirs.

I slipped into the kitchen and made a beeline for the kettle. Two young men I didn't recognize were laughing together as they grabbed a couple of chip bags out of the cupboard. Just my luck, as Darius stalked in after me, my only other company ambled out, leaving me alone with him after all.

"Why am I getting the feeling you're avoiding me?" he asked, propping himself against the kitchen island a few feet from where I stood.

"I don't know," I retorted. "Because your ego is so overblown you assume everything anyone does is about you?"

"Hmm. Is it really the size of my *ego* you've had on your mind?"

"I haven't really spent much time thinking about you at all," I said flippantly, which was a total lie. Although mostly I'd been thinking about punching him in his cocky face.

Darius tsked his tongue. "I heard you've been naughty. Sneaking off in the middle of the night."

I tensed despite my best intentions. I didn't think Lucan had reported my stealthy excursion to his father, since Marcel hadn't hassled me about it, but maybe it wasn't a surprise that he'd mentioned it to his brothers.

"I thought your father would prefer it if I wasn't seen walking in and out the door more than necessary."

"I doubt he expected you to be quite that stealthy. Where did you have to go so urgently anyway?"

"Where do you think?" I'd had plenty of time to come up with a cover story now. I glanced over my shoulder at him, arching my eyebrows. "You've made it *very* clear that I'm not welcome here. My brother isn't going to open his door to me any time soon, and I don't think I'd want to go back under his roof anyway. So I'm doing what I can to figure out a new situation for myself. And the kinds of dealings that happen in the middle of the night are all I really know, as you should probably understand."

Darius grunted with obvious skepticism. "Your brother would really disown you that totally?"

"You don't know Ezra," I said. "Although from what

I've been hearing, you probably should be able to figure out how ruthless he can be."

There wasn't much Darius could say to that. He opened a drawer and took out a tea towel that he whipped against his hand with a smack that made my nerves jump —and not totally in an unpleasant way. A traitorous part of me immediately started imagining him spanking me with it.

But Darius had other ideas. "I think you've been here long enough that you should start earning your keep," he said. "You seem to be getting a lot of use out of this kitchen. Let's see you pitch in by wiping down this floor."

Oh, he was going to go there, was he? I glanced down at the glossy gray tiles. "They already look pretty clean to me."

"Trying to weasel your way out of repaying what you owe us?"

I glowered at him. "No, just making an observation." An idea clicked in my head, a way I could make this more torture for him than it was for me. I snatched the towel from his hands and dipped it under the tap. "If it'll make you happy."

"Very happy," he shot back with a broad grin.

I knelt down on my hands and knees near the wall, keeping my distance but staying within his view, and tugged my dress so my knees wouldn't mash the fabric into the floor. Then I started scrubbing.

As I swept my hand back and forth over the nearest tiles, I let my hips sway. My ass rose a little higher in the air, then a little higher still. From the corner of my eyes, I saw Darius lick his lips.

"That's right," he said. "Exactly where you should be—down on your knees."

"I definitely don't want to know what *you're* imagining right now," I said, but I let a little breathiness creep into my tone.

Darius shifted his weight as if his pants had gotten tighter. Ha.

"I'll imagine whatever I want," he murmured. "And you should be imagining all the things I could do to you while you're bent over like that, if you deserved it. I'd have you swaying twice that hard."

"Then I'm not scrubbing hard enough." I put more umph into the strokes of my arm, rocking my whole body back and forth just slightly. Without looking, I could feel Darius's gaze glued to my every movement.

He came around the island so he was closer to me. I shuffled forward as if I needed to anyway to get to the next tiles, giving him an even more direct view of my ass. The door was still open—this wasn't exactly the most dignified position for someone to look in and see me in. But I didn't really give a shit what any of the Hell Kickers thought of me.

"Such a natural," Darius teased, but his tone was turning heated. I smiled inwardly.

And now, while he was distracted, I could do a different sort of prying of my own. "What's the deal with that Griffin guy?" I asked in an offhand way, giving my hips another sway.

Darius took a second to answer. "What about him?"

"I met him when I arrived. He seemed tight with your dad. *Really* tight. Is he collaborating with you and your brothers on the second tier of leadership or something?"

The oldest Rosano brother scoffed. "Not likely. He's just a suck-up who cares more about impressing people than actually getting a job done properly."

It seemed like Griffin's efforts had been succeeding, from what I'd seen. Darius obviously didn't consider him a threat, though. He didn't sound like he had any clue the guy had been lying about him to Marcel, but I didn't see any reason to inform him. Why should I lend this asshole a hand?

"If you think that dork is going to be your Prince Charming and get you out of this, you're sniffing around the wrong tree," Darius went on. "While you're here, *we* own you, and no one else is staking any claim."

Oh, really. I owned myself just fine. I restrained the urge to roll my eyes and decided it was time to up my game.

"I'm getting my dress dirty on this floor," I grumbled, and paused to tuck folds of the fabric right into my panties to hold it off the ground. The gesture exposed most of my thighs. Then I went back to scrubbing and swaying away, subtly shaking my ass in Darius's direction.

He sucked in a breath. Then the rasp of a zipper startled me. He reached right into his jeans and fisted the erection that'd been enclosed beneath.

"You know what I'm going to do?" he said, his voice going even lower and darker—and, to my annoyance, sending a shiver straight to my sex. "I'm going to jack off to the sight of you on your hands and knees doing my bidding, and then I'm going to come right on your ass."

I chose not to answer. Partly because the rubbing sound of his palm pumping over his rigid cock was setting off a deeper wave of heat inside me. It was a good thing I hadn't totally exposed my panties, because the crotch had just dampened. Fuck.

He shouldn't affect me like this. And maybe it was time I taught him a thing or two about messing with Anthea Noble.

The new idea that sparked in my head brought me up short, but only for a moment. A slight smile curled my lips. It would serve him fucking right. Let's see if he bared that dick anywhere near me ever again.

I wiggled my ass and wiped at the floor, giving him a good show. "You obviously don't find enough women who can put out if you're that desperate."

He chuckled, his breath getting rough. "I just take my opportunities as they come, and this is a fantastic one. You don't seem to mind all that much, Lady Noble."

"Guess I'm not that much of a lady, then." The pace of his strokes was speeding up. I might not have a lot of time. But then I heard what I'd been waiting for to solidify my plan: distant voices down the hall, getting a little louder as they moved closer.

I peeked coyly over at Darius, getting an eyeful of his admittedly impressive cock clenched in his pumping hand. I might have salivated a little, but I held my focus.

"You could come on my ass," I said, "but wouldn't you like my mouth even more?"

Darius's eyes grew heavy-lidded. "You want this, do you? Or maybe you just want to keep your pretty dress clean. Either way, it works for me. Come and get it."

I crawled over to him, knowing that would turn him on even more. Better if he didn't think too hard about my momentary obedience.

As I rose up on my knees, his breath caught. He gripped the base of his erection, offering his cock to me. I wrapped my lips around the head, the musky flavor provoking a flash of desire I tuned out. He thrust forward to drive farther into my mouth—

And I chomped down.

I didn't bite *hard*. I wasn't looking to tear his dick right off, as much as he might have deserved it. But I dug my teeth into the sensitive flesh just below the head of his cock firmly enough that he yelped loud enough to wake the dead.

As I yanked back from him—and he heaved himself away from me—a shout of alarm sounded down the hall. Darius swore through his teeth, pained and furious, and stuffed himself back into his pants. Making sure his underlings didn't find out what'd happened to him was his first priority over payback.

Which gave me time to shoot him a sunny smirk, scramble to my feet, and dash out of the room just before his defenders hustled in.

I jogged back upstairs, deciding I was going to hole up in my bedroom after all—once I'd barricaded the door. Because I didn't for one second believe that payback wouldn't be coming. I'd only ensured it'd be delayed for a little while.

I shoved a chair under the doorknob. Then, unable to help myself, I flopped down on my bed, shoved my hand under my skirt, and fingered myself until I was coming with a gasp and doing my best not to fixate on the taste of Darius lingering on my tongue.

TEN

Felix

THE NEW CHICK who'd started hanging around the Hell Kickers headquarters was definitely my type. But then, I had a pretty broad type. Give me perky boobs and curvy hips, and not a whole lot else mattered. I'd take 'em blond or brunette, pale or dark…

As I looked at the tan, raven-haired cutie I'd ambled over to, an image flashed through my mind of bright red hair and lightly freckled skin. I shook it away, restraining a grimace. Fuck, no, Anthea Noble was not invading my head right now. I was done with that cock-tease unless I could get her properly at my mercy.

I leaned against the wall at an angle that showed off the musculature beneath my tailored linen button up and flashed the new chick a grin. "So, you've been liking what you see around here?"

She peeked at me through her eyelashes. "Definitely

some things. Do you, like, help run things and everything with your dad? That must be pretty exciting."

I couldn't remember the last time Dad had actually asked for *my* advice. Darius was the commanding one, Lucan was the smart one, and I... I was the guy who actually enjoyed the lifestyle our family had created for ourselves. They knew I'd step up however they needed if they needed me, though.

"Sure," I said smoothly. "It's a complicated business, but someone's got to keep everything chugging along. I do carve out time to relax, of course. Can't be all work and no play."

She gave me a coy smile. "That's good to hear. Which are you up for right now?"

I motioned toward the stairs. "I could give you an insider's tour of the place. Maybe that'll include a little of both."

She giggled her agreement and pranced along beside me as we meandered through the halls. Sooner rather than later, I made sure we ended up in my bedroom. She shed her clothes like they were on fire, and her curves were even perkier naked.

I should have been hard. I should have been ready to plunge right into her and erase the memory of a different woman's hand on my dick. But even when the chick—whose name I'd either never gotten or not bothered to remember, I realized—bent down with her boobs swaying to swipe her tongue over my cock, it didn't rise any higher than half-mast.

What the hell was wrong with me? I spun the woman around so her ass was to me, rubbed my partial erection against her butt while I slapped her across one cheek. She was creaming, drenched for me, and my damned cock still wouldn't stiffen.

I did have a reputation to keep up. No fucking way was I going to let word get around that Felix had gone floppy. I reached into the drawer under my platform bed and got out one of the dildos in my collection of toys that usually came in handy when I was playing with more than one woman at a time.

I didn't say anything to the chick, couldn't even tell if she'd realized I'd decided to get her off with silicone instead of flesh. By the time I was done thrusting the thing into her and fondling her with my other hand, she'd sagged with so much pleasure I wasn't sure she even remembered who *I* was.

Maybe that was okay. I tossed the toy aside for washing and swatted her shoulder. "The tour is over. But I might see you around again."

"Hmm, I could go for that."

She did a bit of a reverse strip tease as she tugged her clothes back on, and I pretended to be eating up the show. In the back of my mind, Anthea leaned into me in the coat closet, her hand closing around my shaft…

Just like that, my cock jumped to attention. I bit back a growl of frustration.

When the chick had left, I paced my room for a few minutes. This wasn't good. Having fun with the women who fawned over any hint of gang power was one of the few things in this life I *was* really good at. Anthea wasn't going to ruin that for me. No fucking way.

Why the hell was Dad even letting her stick around all

this time? She'd already spied on us once, when she was a lot less capable than she clearly was now. Was he out of his mind?

I decided abruptly that I'd better find out. Sure, I didn't generally talk strategy with Dad, but I *was* still his son. If he had some grand plan going on that involved the Noble interloper, then I should know about it, shouldn't I? I deserved to be filled in on why he was making us put up with the treacherous bitch.

He was holding court in his office, like usual. I heard voices through the door and shifted on my feet as I waited, knowing he wouldn't like me interrupting. Especially when I didn't have anything he'd see as urgent to discuss.

I strolled down the hall, halting when I realized I'd almost reached Anthea's room, and spun around to stalk back. Thankfully by the time I'd approached the office again, the two lackeys who'd been consulting with the old man were heading out.

I brushed past them and strode into the office, channeling a little Darius, because why not? Dad seemed to like him best, so my big bro was obviously doing something right.

Dad's eyebrows rose from behind his desk as he watched me cross the room. He set aside the paper he'd been writing on and folded his hands together. "Felix. What brings you here, son?"

He probably figured I wanted permission to throw a house party or something. To be fair, that was closer to my usual M.O.

I rested my hands on the back of an armchair, grappling with the best way to bring up the subject. I settled for straightforward but relatively neutral. "I was just wondering how long we're going to be housing that Noble asshole's sister. She seems to be making herself at home here."

Dad waved off the remark, leaning back in his chair. "I think it's good having her under our roof. Ezra might not have wanted to deal with her, but I doubt he's completely detached from his sense of family. If we need leverage, we've got her right here. If we want to prod some information out of her, it's a lot easier with her where we can control her."

How much had he actually interacted with Anthea for him to think controlling her would be remotely easy? She'd probably be out the fucking window, never to return, the second she caught the slightest whiff that he was heading in that direction. Hell, that might even be why she'd already been slipping out the window to start setting up alternate arrangements.

No, that would be assuming that she didn't have nefarious purposes of her own here. That she actually needed shelter instead of her sob story being a gambit.

"That makes sense," I said, because it was always good to pay a compliment before you said any kind of criticism. "But what if she's digging up information about *us*? That whole story about Ezra could be fake. We know he's had it in for us. And it's not like she's any stranger to sneaking around under false pretenses."

Dad's hard-edged face darkened with a frown. "I knew you boys all got a little attached to her, but I didn't think you expected so much from her that you'd see her getting married to someone else as a betrayal. You never even talked about her after her last visit."

Why would he think I meant that kind of betrayal?

"No," I said. "I mean her last visit. The whole thing— Holly must have told you about it."

Dad only looked more puzzled. "Holly told me that Anthea left early because she wasn't feeling well and wanted to be at home," he said. "Do you think she was pretending about that? Did the three of you have some kind of falling out with her? You really need to put those kinds of silly teenage squabbles behind you after all this time, Felix."

Frustration bubbled up inside me alongside my shock. He didn't have to be so fucking *patronizing* about it.

And did he really not know? Holly hadn't told him? Had she thought he'd blame her for not noticing Anthea's treachery sooner or something? Or maybe she'd been worried he'd get angry with the messenger in general and assumed one of us would broach the subject with him, saving her the hassle.

Shit.

I groped for the words to convincingly explain that the woman whose plea for help he'd apparently bought into had actually been a sixteen-year-old lying, conniving cunt all that time ago, but before I could get out more than a, "Well…" Dad's new favorite lackey burst into the room.

The guy didn't even knock, for fuck's sake. He pushed past the door with his bulky shoulders and marched over to Dad's desk like he belonged there, his beady eyes skimming over me like *I* didn't.

Griffin, that was his name, like a fucking mythological beast. He looked like some kind of creature, all right.

"I need to touch base about something, Marcel," he said in a low urgent voice, switching to ignoring me completely.

I cleared my throat, but Dad made a dismissive gesture at me. "I think you've said enough. If you see anything that's a real cause for concern, bring it to me then."

I opened my mouth to protest and realized I *hadn't* actually seen anything. That was, other than Anthea dishing back what we threw at her as fast as she could, but I didn't think Dad wanted to hear about that.

He'd care if I caught her in some kind of scheme. I'd just have to keep my eyes peeled. Hell, maybe if I was the one who nailed her—for a crime, not the other way, although I wouldn't mind breaking her like that too—he wouldn't look at me like a total putz.

I nodded and stalked out of the room. I was just starting down the hall when one of the regular minions from the household ducked out of Dad's lounge room a couple doors farther along.

His head was ducked, his curly brown hair spilling over his forehead, his stout frame a little hunched. What was *his* name? Something with a B… Brandon? Brent?

Lucan would have known. Lucan had a hard-on about picking up every underling's name no matter how inconsequential they were. He said it was good leadership or some bullshit like that.

Br-whatever had a hardcover book tucked under his arm. He glanced both ways down the hall and spotted me.

From his stance, I expected him to startle, but he just headed my way as if he wasn't bothered at all.

"Your dad asked me to grab this for him," he said, indicating the book.

Great, so Dad was counting on even doofuses like this more than me. I wouldn't take that as an insult.

"You might need to give him a few minutes," I said tartly. "He's in a meeting."

Then I strode off as if I had somewhere much more important to be. Which I supposed I did. I needed to be wherever I could spark the fuse that'd lead to Anthea Noble's destruction.

ELEVEN

Anthea

I WASN'T ACTUALLY a prisoner in the Rosanos' brownstone. No one stopped me when I meandered out the front door the following evening. If asked, I would have said I was looking to grab a bite to eat rather than cooking tonight, and since Brant had come through in pawning Clyde's trinkets, I even had the cash to support that story.

What I actually did was walk in the direction of the nearest shopping strip on a winding route for a few minutes until I'd played out all my tricks to confirm I wasn't being followed, then circle back around and flag a cab. Mick had stopped by the brownstone again this afternoon. I'd seen which direction his car had arrived in, and I was gambling that he'd drive off in the same direction.

The cabbie gave me an odd look when I told him just to park a few blocks down from the brownstone and let the meter run, but he was getting paid for nothing, so he didn't complain. I handed over a twenty to show I was good for it. It was only a few minutes more before the subtly sleek silver Hyundai cruised past us.

"Follow that car," I told the cabbie. "Just don't get too close."

He shrugged. "Whatever you say, lady. You figure he's cheating on you or something?"

I smiled tightly. "Something like that, yeah."

The Hyundai headed east, winding through the Brooklyn streets and on into Queens. I dropped another twenty on the front passenger seat so the cabbie wouldn't get antsy about the length of the journey. Finally, we eased to a stop when the silver car pulled into the driveway of a modest but pretty neo-Tudor style house in Kew Gardens.

It wasn't a mansion like the Noble home in Paradise City or as posh as the Rosanos' brownstone, but I'd bet it'd cost a good chunk of change. From the pink bike with sparkly streamers tipped over in the small, otherwise neat front yard, Mick was a family man. Was this why he'd have screwed over the Rosanos—had he taken on too much debt and now he was struggling to stay afloat? He wouldn't be the first person it'd happened to.

If that was the case and he'd been too embarrassed to admit it to his boss, he might even have started his downward descent by borrowing money from other crooks. Crooks who'd threatened severe enough consequences that murdering his colleagues to steal a shipment of goods and the money for them had seemed like the better option.

That was all speculation, though. I hadn't seen any

actual evidence. My brother had sent me to take care of this task because he knew I'd be thorough—he knew I'd make sure the right people paid.

The residents at a house on the other side of the street were just heading out to their car—their voices carried through the window with comments about the dinner they were looking forward to. Perfect. I waited until they'd driven away, paid the cabbie the rest of the fare along with a generous tip, and slipped over to the shadows next to the recently vacated garage. In the thickening dusk, no one would notice me there.

I watched Mick's house for as long as seemed wise, about an hour. No one else drove up to the home. Various cars cruised by along the street, but I didn't notice any that seemed to slow down or otherwise focus on his place. Mick didn't emerge from the house again, although toward the end of the hour a middle-aged woman came out with a girl who looked around ten, who grumbled as she dragged her bike down the driveway.

They didn't seem worried about anything, but of course, that wasn't proof one way or another either. At least I had some additional data I could bring to bear in later investigations. Maybe I could use the second burner phone I'd hidden in my things to contact Wylder and see if that techie friend of his, Gideon, would dig up any financial records that'd give me a sense of what pressures the Rosanos' lead smuggler might be facing.

I walked until I reached a busier street where I could hail another cab and hopped into the back. When the driver asked, "Where to?" I opened my mouth to give him the Rosanos' address and then hesitated. A sudden urge gripped me.

"Orvil Street," I said, drawing up a mental image of the map I'd peered at yesterday. "Orvil and Fifth."

"No problem."

We drove back into Brooklyn, reaching the big shopping strip down the west end of the borough. Orvil branched off from the busier street with a variety of shops of its own. Many of them had already closed for the night, but I spotted some activity farther down the street, furtive movements that set my nerves on the alert.

I got out of the cab by Fifth Avenue and slunk down Orvil, sticking close to the storefronts. Men were hustling in and out of a small office building with a shoe store on the first floor. I didn't recognize any of them in the darkness, but I spotted the unmistakable bulge of pistols shoved in the backs of a few pairs of jeans.

A prickle of apprehension ran down my back. I eased right back into a nearby doorway to watch from that relative shelter.

A truck was parked a few feet down from the office building. Some of the men were carrying crates from it into the building, and others were carrying boxes and bags out, like it was moving day and they were handling both the old and new owners' possessions.

"Where did Griffin want this shit?" one of the guys called to another, just barely loud enough for me to make out the words.

The second guy motioned to the truck. "Stick it at the back. They'll sort through it later."

This was part of the operation that prick had been

discussing with Marcel, then. Why had the two of them been so secretive about it? Setting up a new place of business operations wasn't that out of the ordinary.

Then a few of the guys barged out through the office doors not carrying boxes but ushering a couple of men who looked worse for wear in the hazy glow of the streetlamps. One had a bruise on his jaw and another a cut on his temple that was still seeping blood.

"Go on, then," one of the Hell Kickers said, shoving them away. "There's nothing here for you anymore. You bet on the wrong horse."

One of the men hurried off, but the other stopped in the middle of the street to spin around and sneer at the Hell Kickers. "I don't think so. You'd better believe the Nobles are going to make you pay for this, you fuckers."

A chill washed through me. Those were Noble men— this had been my family's property?

A Hell Kicker lackey raised his gun in a clear threat. "Get the fuck out of here, or you'll end up in the dirt like the guys you used to work with."

The Noble man swore through his teeth but moved on, favoring his leg. I watched him go and then scanned the building more closely. Was that blood spatter on the edge of the front window?

That was what Griffin had meant about Marcel cracking down and showing his strength. He'd leveraged the catastrophe of the deal gone wrong into an excuse to start a war with my brother, starting with taking over what could very well be Ezra's only Brooklyn property. Ezra had been encouraging Dad to expand for a while and overseeing several ventures himself, but he hadn't set down many roots outside our state. That place was probably his flagship in all of New York.

Which meant this was not just a blow but a major one.

I gritted my teeth, my anger burning away the previous chill. If I'd been as hotheaded as my red hair might suggest, I'd have marched over there and given all those pricks a piece of my mind. But I wasn't an idiot. That'd blow my cover and probably get me killed.

One of the Hell Kickers' major long-time allies had supposedly double-crossed them for the first time ever, and just a couple of weeks later, Marcel had launched a strike on the Nobles' territory? Had he bought into Mick's story that thoroughly, not even considering that Ezra might be telling the truth when he'd insisted he'd lost everything in the deal too?

Or maybe Marcel had been in on the scheme after all. He might have orchestrated it with Mick to give him an excuse to push the Nobles out of Brooklyn and maybe take over even more of our territory, and just be pretending with Griffin that he felt wronged. His comments to Mick about their losses could simply be in reference to Hell Kicker men he hadn't expected to die in the scheme.

Or it could be that Griffin and Mick had conspired together to push Marcel in this direction, and the Hell Kickers' boss was none the wiser.

But Ezra was going to make them pay. How much Noble blood had they spilled already? They weren't going to get away with it—not under my brother's watch, and not under mine.

I watched for a little longer, but I couldn't tell what the Hell Kickers might be setting up in their new offices from this distance in the dark, and I couldn't see any way to get closer without revealing myself. Then I headed back to the brownstone on foot, stopping only to grab a burger from a fast-food place so I had fuel for all the thinking I needed to do. As I walked on, chewing pensively, I barely noticed the bustle of Fifth Avenue restaurant goers I passed.

Whether Marcel was in on the gambit or simply being duped into seeing Ezra as the villain, he should have known better. He'd been friends with my dad for how long? And the first thing that went wrong, he jumped straight into war. Some fucking loyalty.

No doubt the only reason he'd taken me in was in the hopes that he could use me somehow toward that cause. Ha. Little did he know. If I found out he had been behind the disaster with the Noble deal, I wouldn't hesitate to take him down along with whichever lackeys had supported him in carrying it out.

The Hell Kickers could crumble right to the ground for all I cared. Let the roof collapse on his sons' heads for good measure.

The walk through the cooling night air dulled only some of my wrath. When the brownstone came into view up ahead, I allowed myself the indulgence of glaring at it from a distance for just a moment before schooling my expression into placid gratitude for my approach.

I didn't stay placid for long. I'd only just walked in the front door and made it to the bottom of the stairs when Darius stepped forward, catching me by the elbow.

"Let go of me," I snapped, yanking at my arm. I had no patience for dealing with his crap right now.

He held fast, his grip and his gaze like steel. "You're coming with me," he said in an equally deadly voice, and ushered me up the stairs, past the second-floor hall, and on up toward the apartment he shared with his brothers.

TWELVE

Anthea

I'D NEVER WANTED to set foot in this room again. Never wanted to see it, never wanted to even *think* about it. But when I tried to dig my heels in outside the doorway to the common room the Rosano brothers' shared in the section of the third floor they'd claimed as a private apartment, Darius just dragged me in, forcefully enough that I had to stumble after him or I'd have tripped. I guessed I was lucky he hadn't slung me over his shoulder caveman-style.

He slammed the door behind us and shoved me against the wall next to it. Over his shoulder, I could see that the common room between the guys' bedrooms looked pretty much the same as it always had. A leather sofa was flanked by matching armchairs facing a massive entertainment system. A desk and a couple of bookshelves now overflowing with volumes stood across from it.

They even had a little kitchenette setup for if they got too lazy to go downstairs, with a set of cupboards, a mini fridge, and a microwave next to a four-person dining table. A huge Persian rug covered most of the hardwood floor.

It smelled the same and yet not, the leather and hardwood mingling with a few cologne notes that'd stayed the same and others that had matured with the men who wore them. The crisply spicy scent wafting off Darius right now wasn't the same stuff he'd slapped on his neck as a teen.

I focused on him looming over me, pinning me against the wall between his braced hands. If I was looking at the man he was now, it was easier to tune out the memories tugging at the corners of my mind.

"Where the fuck have you been?" he snarled.

I blinked at him, holding on to my cool. Too bad for him I was still too pissed off at his family and the people they employed to be intimidated or otherwise affected by his closeness. Even if a trace of his most intimate flavor seemed to briefly waver across my tongue.

Right, he had good reasons to be pissed off at *me* that had nothing to do with where I'd gone.

"I went out to get dinner," I said, glad I had actually eaten something on the way back so that my stomach wouldn't gurgle and betray me. "I didn't realize I needed to ask your permission to feed myself."

"You were gone for a long time."

I shot him a tight smile. "Keeping track of my comings and goings so closely, were you? I didn't realize you cared so much about little ol' me. Maybe I wanted to enjoy a very leisurely dinner somewhere other than here after the incredibly enthusiastic welcome I've gotten. There's something to be said for peace and quiet."

My sarcasm about my welcome added a bite to my voice. Darius scowled at me and pushed away, stalking toward the sofa and then back.

There was no sign of his brothers. I wasn't sure if that was a good thing or a bad thing. I was only dealing with him, but he had no one to temper his rage. No one to worry about putting on a responsible front for.

His voice from years ago rose up in the back of my head. *It's a lot of pressure, you know. Of course I'm supposed to take over when Dad's ready—and I want to. But everything I do around the people we work with counts toward how they'll see me as a leader. And they're always around. It's only in here that I can relax a little… but I've got to be strong for Lucan and Felix too.*

We'd been sitting on the sofa; I could almost feel the smooth leather against my bare shins where I'd curled my legs up on the cushion. My heart had beat faster at his confession—at the fact that he'd confided in me.

You don't have to impress me, I said. *I don't count. Even if I was the oldest, my dad would never even* think *of asking me to do anything all that important for the business.*

And oh, the way my pulse had fluttered when Darius had shot me a warm grin. *I don't have to put on a show for you, Lady Noble, but that doesn't mean you don't count. I'd say that means you do, a lot.*

All those fucking lies I'd eaten up like the inexperienced teenage girl I was.

"You'd better not be fucking lying to me," Darius said now, prowling closer again.

"Or you'll what?" I retorted. "Let me lick your dick again? That went so well for you last time."

I shouldn't have mentioned that, not in here. Because suddenly I was remembering a few nights after that conversation, when the guys had all squeezed onto the sofa around me, when a hand had rested casually on my knee or my wrist for several seconds at a time, an escalation of the closeness and the tentative touches that'd been stirring up my hormones and my hopes since I'd first arrived for the summer.

It'd been Felix who'd made the first real move. Felix who'd shut off the movie with a sly glint in his eyes and then leaned in to kiss me, as confidently as if we'd made out a dozen times before. I could taste his lips as clearly as I could hear the sounds of protest and the hasty discussion that'd followed.

You can't just— You don't get to just decide *that she's with you*, Darius had insisted, all wounded authority.

I thought we agreed that we weren't going to make any moves unless she did first, Lucan had put in, his face flushed.

The thought that they'd talked about this, that they might all have *wanted* to make a move, had heated me from head to toe. And somehow sixteen-year-old virginal me had found the bravado to announce, *Who says I have to decide to be with just one of you anyway? What if I like all of you?*

Darius shattered the memory, blocking my view of the sofa with his brawny form. "You'd better believe that by the time we're done here, I'll be getting an apology for that and a whole lot more."

I couldn't hold back a snort, my anger mingling with the anguish from seven years ago into a dizzying mix.

"Oh, I think if we're adding up who's done more wrong to who, I'm not the one who's in the red."

I'd made it so fucking easy for them back then. Handed myself to them on a platter thinking I'd won a prize. But I'd been the prize: Anthea Noble, only daughter of the head of the Nobles and their dad's close friend. Letting them touch me, letting them *fuck* me—Darius and then Felix inside me, Lucan in my inexperienced mouth gasping like I was the second coming, pun not intended.

All their murmured words and tender caresses had been nothing but a stupid vicious pretense to be able to claim my virginity between them like some kind of trophy. My hands clenched at my sides.

Darius's face had tightened alongside my fists. "Are you kidding me? After all the shit you and your brother have pulled, you're going to make it sound like *you're* the real victim?"

"All the shit *we've* pulled?" I snapped before I could catch the words. "We weren't the ones who staged a shootout to justify a goddamn war."

Confusion flickered across Darius's expression, and I clamped my mouth shut. Shit. I shouldn't have said that much, shouldn't have revealed that I didn't believe the story about the deal gone wrong.

"What the hell did you just say?" he demanded. "Who staged what? What war?"

As if his father wouldn't have bragged to him about the recent victory.

"Never mind," I said coldly, groping for my composure. I wasn't going to find it in this room. I turned toward the door. "I just wanted to see if you were even listening to me."

Darius caught me by the upper arm and yanked me across the room before my fingers could close around the doorknob. I staggered on the rug and spun around.

"No way," he said, jabbing his forefinger at me, his eyes blazing now and his voice gone rough. "We're not falling for your bullshit again. You're up to something here, just like you always are. You think we don't know you hooked that old fucker into marriage just so you could murder him and bring the business back home? All cold calculation down to the goddamned bone. I *see* you."

An icy tremor ran through me at his mention of Clyde. Something in me cracked right through. Maybe it'd been on the verge of fracturing for days now, since the first moment the Rosano brothers had descended on me like a pack of hyenas looking to see what they could scavenge from their past wreckage.

My insides seared with white-hot rage, but my voice came out deathly frigid. I advanced on Darius, unable to stop it from shaking with my next words.

"I'd have given *anything* not to marry 'that old fucker,' you jackass. Do you want me to show you the presents he gave me, the scars that still haven't healed? Just a small assortment of the worst of the smacks and burns and jabs I took over those five years. And that's not even getting into the bruises you could never see: hearing the shit he hurled at me every day, having to bow to his sick whims so that my dad wouldn't show up and kill *me* for screwing up *his* deal. I'd throw away every bit of my inheritance if it meant spending one less day under that asshole's roof."

Darius's jaw had gone slack. He'd really thought that I'd happily gone along with the marriage? For fuck's sake.

I was too far gone now to hold back the rest of the words searing up my throat while he stood there in startled silence. "But you know what, it could have been worse. It'd have hurt more if I'd expected better, but I knew what I was being sold into from the start. In five years, he never gutted me the way the three of you did. I was always perfectly aware that I was nothing to him. With you…"

As my tirade petered out, exhaustion rolled over me. Darius swallowed audibly, his forehead furrowing. "Anthea…"

I waved my hand in dismissal. "Whatever. It was years ago. We were all kids or not much more than that. But you know what happened to the last man who used me as a punching bag. If you or either of your brothers hurts me again, just imagine what I'll do to *you*."

When I strode past him this time, he didn't lunge fast enough to stop me. I hurtled down the stairs and rushed to my bedroom, but even as I set my purse down on the bed, I knew I couldn't stand to stay here. Empty-handed, I swiveled and marched right out again, back to the stairwell, farther down, to the first floor and then descending into the cooler dimness of the basement.

I didn't really know where I was going, only that I wanted to be away, somewhere none of them could quickly find me.

I hadn't meant to say so much to Darius. I hadn't meant to lay it all out. I couldn't even say the confession had felt good. It was like I'd spat up acid and now my insides were burning from my stomach all the way to my throat.

The basement was a maze of tiled, low-ceilinged hallways, a huge home gym, a wine cellar, and about a million general storage rooms. Probably at least one of which was reserved for torture, knowing how gangs like this operated.

Shouts and sporadic laughter echoed through the halls alongside strange whuffs and thumps. I rounded a corner and then drew back, seeing a few of the younger lackeys including the guy who'd fenced my valuables for me—Brant—brandishing Nerf guns of all things.

I guessed that was one way to get in some practice when they couldn't shoot off real guns around here without a neighbor potentially calling the cops.

As I watched from the shadows, the guys faced off. One foam ball blasted Brant in the shoulder; his two shots went wild. His companions cackled and cuffed him on the shoulder, mingling reassurances with insults the way men liked to do.

"Just not my thing," he said with a shake of his head.

I pulled back through the nearest doorway as they headed toward me. The other guys strode on ahead, and Brant brought up the rear. He paused just before he reached my doorway, waiting until his colleagues had turned a corner up ahead, and raised his toy gun. I was standing at just the right angle to see the ball bounce right off the little light switch on the wall twenty feet away, flicking its position.

He chuckled quietly to himself as if he wasn't actually

surprised by his accuracy and strode on through the now total dark.

Silence fell over the basement. I was alone—totally, blissfully alone. I drew in a few breaths, rubbing my arms as I wandered through the room, and sank down with my back to a stack of cardboard boxes.

I'd just sit here for a little while until I felt ready to face the rest of humanity again. Until the part of me that'd cracked had sealed itself up again. Darius never needed to see *that* side of me again.

I raised my knees and leaned forward to rest my forehead against them. My eyelids slid shut. Before I realized it would happen, I was slipping away from the agony of that confrontation the surest way my body knew how, drifting off into sleep.

THIRTEEN

Darius

I WAS the heir to the Hell Kickers and the Rosano family legacy. Second in command to Dad, giving direct orders to dozens of underlings... I shouldn't have been blindsided by *anything* that crossed my path. It was my job to be prepared for any possible shit that anyone could throw at me.

But I hadn't been prepared for Anthea Noble after all. Not raging at me with so much pain shimmering in her storm-gray eyes that it'd burned a hole in my gut.

What the hell had she even been talking about at the end there? She'd talked as if *we'd* wronged her in some way —not with how we'd treated her recently but the last time she was here, when we were kids. How did that make any sense?

And what she'd said about her husband... The memory of her taut voice made my hands close into fists. I believed what she'd said about his abuse. I believed it enough that in spite of all the reasons I had to be angry with her, I wanted to drag him out of his grave to kill him all over again.

Did I have reasons to be angry with her? Other than for chomping on my fucking dick, which I couldn't help thinking still required some groveling. This whole situation felt as if it'd turned on its head, and I no longer knew which direction was up.

Maybe she'd messed with *my* head again despite my best efforts, and none of this was really all that confusing.

As I rubbed my temple as if I could shove my thoughts into more coherent order, Lucan strode in. He glanced at me and frowned in a clear question.

He might be able to sort out what I'd just heard. Maybe we all should talk. It'd been all of us together when the crap had gone down seven years ago. Both of my brothers had as much of a stake in this as I did, really.

"Find Felix," I said. "We need to toss the ball around out back."

Lucan arched an eyebrow, but he headed off to round up our little brother anyway. I went into my bedroom and retrieved the football we'd doctored with glow-in-the-dark strips for this purpose.

As a kid, I'd always found it easiest to hash things out with my brothers when we were in the backyard throwing the ball around. It brought a rhythm to the conversation, a sense of connection and collaboration, and focusing on the catching and tossing stopped anyone from getting too worked up about the topics of conversation.

As those topics had gotten more serious, we'd stopped going out during the day when you never knew which underlings would be hanging around out there too. But at night, we were pretty much guaranteed to have the space to ourselves. And catching the ball based mostly on sound and little streaks of light brought an extra challenge to the exercise.

Apparently Felix hadn't been difficult to find. He and Lucan were already standing by the back door when I reached it, Lucan looking thoughtfully alert as usual and Felix bemused.

"Really?" he said, nodding to the football. "When are you going to grow out of that?"

I glowered at him. "It works. Now come on before I have you catch it with your face."

As expected at nine o'clock at night, the backyard was empty. The only light was cast by the security lamp over the back deck mingling with the glow in the windows on our house and the one next door. We walked across the patio and past the old elm tree to the open area near the garage. Lucan, ever cautious, peeked into the garage itself to confirm that no one was going to be eavesdropping from in there.

I was fine with his wariness. This wasn't exactly business-business, but it wasn't a conversation I wanted publicized either.

I turned the football in my hands as we spread out in a vague triangle and tossed it to Felix without warning, as repayment for being mouthy. He snorted, catching it easily, and flicked it on toward Lucan. "What's this about?" he asked.

"Anthea," I said, and felt the vibe in the yard turn tense with just those three syllables.

"What's she done now?" Felix muttered in a way that made me wonder what she'd already done to him that I didn't know about. Hopefully he hadn't made the mistake of trying to stick his dick in her mouth.

I caught the ball when Lucan heaved it my way and paused for a second to gather my words. Then I tossed it onward. "I had a little chat with her tonight. She said some things… It's making me want to be sure of what happened the last time she was here."

"Which things in particular?" Lucan asked.

"Holly said she caught Anthea going through Dad's papers, right? Taking pictures of them and stuff. Did we ever come across any other indication that she was out to undermine the family? I don't remember anyone else mentioning catching her at anything like that. Or any incidents based on whatever information she might have passed on from spying."

Lucan shrugged. "She was careful about it. The only reason we know is because Holly caught her. I assumed Dad took into account what Anthea was likely to have seen and adjusted whatever plans he needed to so that there was no chance anyone could interfere with key operations."

I could only vaguely decipher Felix's expression in the dimness, but his voice came out rough enough to show his discomfort. "Dad doesn't know. He *didn't* know."

Lucan's head jerked around, his toss to me going wide in his shock. I lunged to the side to grab the ball out of the air before it thumped into the fence.

"What do you mean?" Lucan demanded. "Of course

Dad knew. Holly probably told him before she even told us. She was his wife."

"Well, we know what a rare and exalted position that is," Felix said dryly, and then sobered up. "I tried to talk to him about Anthea this afternoon. He's suspicious of her motives for coming here right *now*, sure, but only because of the timing with the recent dust-up with the Nobles. He obviously didn't have any idea that she'd been up to no good in the past."

I frowned, an uneasy weight settling in my gut. "How could he *not* know? Why would Holly have told us and not him? She knew it was a problem."

Lucan had knit his brow with a deep enough furrow that it was visible in the darkness. "She might have figured *we'd* tell him. Safer to let us do it in case he reacted badly."

"How were we supposed to know we needed to? She never asked us to." My frown tightened into a scowl. Our stepmom at the time hadn't struck me as all that nervous when she'd informed us that she'd sent Anthea packing after catching her intruding in Dad's office.

I brought up the memory of Holly's sharply pretty face framed by that long hair she'd dyed such a pale blond it'd nearly been white. I'd been so pissed off to find out that Anthea had been using us, that she must have been playing seductress to distract us and get easier access to our private rooms, that I hadn't paid a whole lot of attention to Holly's reaction. But I had the vague impression of her seeming triumphant, like she was pleased with herself for catching the spy.

Wouldn't she have wanted to brag to Dad about how she'd helped him, if that was the case? She'd always been wheedling him to tell her more about his business operations so she could offer advice, wanting him to involve her more in all areas of his life. I was pretty sure her hassling him about that stuff was half of the reason he'd divorced her. The other half being that she'd aged out of his preferred range.

"Is it *possible* that she exaggerated what she saw?" I said slowly, giving the ball a slow fling Felix's way. "She got excited enough to threaten Anthea into leaving and crow about it to us, but when it came to telling Dad, she realized that making that kind of accusation about one of his close friends' daughters might be a step too far if she wasn't totally sure what'd gone down?"

"She did like to puff herself up," Felix remarked. "I could picture that."

"I definitely wouldn't say it *isn't* possible," Lucan said. "But if that's what happened, if Holly accused Anthea and she wasn't really doing anything wrong, why didn't Anthea complain to her dad about it and get Abram to sort everything out with Dad? The fact that she kept quiet about it suggests she had something to feel guilty about."

He had a point, but I couldn't shake my growing apprehension. "We don't know what Holly said to her when she kicked her out. And we do know that Abram was kind of a prick. Anthea might not have felt comfortable admitting to him that his friend's wife even thought she'd violated their trust."

If what she'd said about her dad arranging her marriage and being willing to hurt her worse than her husband had if she hadn't stuck with it was true, then it wasn't at all difficult to imagine her balking at running off to tattle.

Lucan let out a faint huff. "This is all speculation. We can't arrive at definite answers this way."

"But it has given us a better idea of what questions we need to ask." I paused and caught the ball when he whipped it my way. "And who we need to ask. Holly's out to pasture. Even if we tracked her down, I don't think she'd admit to exaggerating. The only other person who knows what went down is Anthea."

Felix guffawed. "She hasn't really seemed to be in a confessing mood."

I swallowed thickly. "We haven't really given her a chance to open up, have we?" She'd only said as much as she had tonight because I seemed to have pushed her past her limit. "Maybe we need to set animosities aside and have an open conversation. Find out what her story is about what happened back then."

"So she can lie some more?" Felix muttered.

"So we can at least know what she would say and judge whether it's a lie or not," Lucan put in with a nod. "You're right. That's our best route to get at the truth. And considering how things are going between us and the Nobles, it's probably better we sort that out sooner rather than later."

How things are going… Those words brought back the other thing Anthea had said that'd struck me, the part that'd been buried under my confusion after her outburst. She's said something about us going to war against the Nobles.

"Have any of you heard about Dad making a move to hit back at the Nobles?" I asked abruptly.

Felix rolled his eyes. "Like I'm part of any of Dad's business decisions."

Lucan shook his head. "As far as I know, Dad's still pressing Ezra for an explanation and compensation, but he doesn't want to burn bridges too quickly given the long alliance."

Then we needed to ask Anthea what had made her mention that too. Too many things didn't add up—or if they did, it was to form a picture I didn't like at all.

I tucked the football under my arm. "Let's go hash this out with her now. No time like the present."

We tramped inside, leaving the ball by the back door so I didn't look like a dork carrying it to this interrogation. Anthea wasn't in the kitchen, one of her frequent haunts in the house, but she had said she'd just gotten back from getting dinner.

When we marched up to the guestroom where she'd been staying, we found it empty. A faint whiff of her scent, tart and resiny, lingered in the air, but there was no sign of the woman herself.

"The screen's still in the window," Lucan observed. "She didn't go out on another stealth mission. It'd be early to go sneaking off by that route anyway."

"Her purse is here." Felix walked over to the bed where it lay and shamelessly riffled through it, holding up her phone and wallet before tucking them back inside. "It doesn't seem likely she'd have left the house for regular reasons without that stuff."

The tension in my gut coiled tighter. "Then she's

around here somewhere. It's not that big a house. Come on."

As we hustled out of her room to make a more thorough search of the building, I couldn't shake the memory of her agonized expression as she'd hurled those last words at me. She'd been awfully upset. Without realizing it, I'd stirred up a whole lot of pain.

She hadn't done something stupid in that emotional state, had she? I wanted to think nothing could get the better of Anthea Noble all that easily… but I'd never thought anything could rattle her as much as I'd seen her just an hour ago.

FOURTEEN

Anthea

THE SKY WAS DARK, but colorful lights radiated through the dusk from behind us. Laughter and giddy shrieks carried through the air.

The boys and I stopped at the edge of the beach. I pulled off my sandals, digging my toes into the sand still warm from baking under the only recently-departed July sun. The guys chucked off their own sneakers. My stomach was full of Coney Island funnel cake, a lingering sweetness lacing my lips, and my pulse kept thumping at a fast tempo after our whirlwind journey from ride to ride.

The beach-goers had started to clear out as the sun set. Small groups scattered the sand, leaving the way in front of us perfectly open. The lifeguards were no longer on duty this late, but I was too exhilarated to care. I gazed across the expanse to the lapping waves, drinking in the salt in the warm air, and beamed.

"I'm hot. Let's cool off with a swim."

Darius, only a tiny bit boyish still at eighteen, gave me a typically imperious look. He didn't care about the rules, but— "We didn't bring bathing suits."

His tone might as well have been a dare. I raised my eyebrows at him with a shrug. "Oh, well." Then I darted across the sand, daring the three of them in turn.

I dropped my sandals just beyond the reach of the waves and plunged right into the water in my shorts and halter top. The delicious chill surged around me, tugging at the thin fabric.

Felix was the first to follow me, of course. He plunged into the waves in all his clothes and tossed back his already-soaked hair, grinning at me.

Lucan and Darius seemed to feel the need to show a little more maturity, being a whole two and three years older than their younger brother. They pulled off their shirts to leave by the heap of shoes, but they came. I even caught a smile from serious Lucan as the water closed around his shoulders.

Felix splashed Darius, who got a sly glint in his eyes and walloped a bunch of water right back. Lucan paddled around with leisurely strokes. I eased onto my back, gazing up at the hazy night sky as the waves rocked me into a perfect sense of peace.

When Felix poked my shoulder, I pulled myself straight again. The boys had gathered around me. I could still touch the bottom here between waves, but something about having the three of them watching me in the darkness, all of us slick with seawater, made my heart skip in a very different way from the thrill of the rides.

A swell of emotion propelled the words from my

throat. "This is always my favorite part of the summer. Not Coney Island, I mean. Coming to Brooklyn. Hanging out with you."

Smiles lit all of their faces then, Lucan's broad enough to be easily visible even in the dimness. "It's our favorite part too."

He reached for me—and the water seemed to swallow me up. The past fell away with a dull roar of the surf, and then I was jolting out of the dream into a different darkness.

There was a kink in my neck and an ache in my ass from the hard floor I'd been sitting on, disturbingly uncomfortable after the joy of the memory that'd risen up in my sleep. With nothing but black around me, it took me a second to get my bearings.

Why *was* I sitting on cold tiles with my back against a cardboard surface?

My argument with the Darius of the present day came flooding back into my head, washing away the last shreds of the dream's happiness. That joy had been a lie anyway— part of their cruel seduction.

I rubbed my eyes and shook my head, but I didn't feel much better. If anything, I only felt more disoriented after what I assumed had been a fairly brief doze given the uncomfortable position. While it was dark, I could hear footsteps rapping across the floor upstairs, so it couldn't be too late at night yet.

I pushed myself to my feet and groped my way to the doorway. In the hall, a thin beam of light streamed down from the stairs around the corner. Shaking off the last shreds of sleep, I hurried toward it.

I should go to sleep properly in my actual bed, and maybe in the morning I'd have a clearer idea of where to go from here.

The activity on the first floor grew louder as I eased up the stairs. It sounded like a dozen people were circulating through the rooms at a brisk pace. I paused while still cloaked in shadow, watching a lackey hustle by with a harried expression.

I hadn't seen this much commotion in the Rosanos' house at this hour before. I wasn't sure I'd seen it even in the middle of the day. What was going on? Had something gone wrong?

Were they gearing up to *do* something wrong, even worse than what I'd already witnessed tonight at my family's former business?

I slunk closer, sticking close to the wall and keeping my ears pricked. A woman who prepared meals for the family darted into view from a nearby room and froze in her tracks. I saw why when Darius advanced on her from the opposite direction.

"Well?" he demanded, his stance tensed and his voice rough.

The woman grimaced. "I'm sorry. I haven't seen any sign of her."

"She's got to be around here somewhere. You checked the pantry?"

"Of course. I can look again."

"Right. Do that."

As she scurried off, Darius sighed and swiped his hand over his face. In that moment, he didn't look angry or suspicious. He looked… worried. Maybe even slightly pained.

My stomach flipped over. I'd assumed from the conversation that they were looking for me, because what other "she" in the house would he be determined to track down, but would he really be that concerned about my whereabouts? About *me*?

I propelled myself forward and emerged into the hall. Darius's head jerked up. His expression snapped into a mask of stern authority, but I didn't think I'd mistaken the brief flicker of relief that'd passed through his eyes in the first instant his gaze had rested on me.

"Where the fuck have you been?" he growled, but at the same time that gaze was sweeping over me from head to toe as if checking for… injuries? What the hell did he *think* I'd been doing?

"I wanted to be sure I'd get some time alone," I said. "The basement seemed like my best bet. Then I accidentally drifted off. It's been a long day. What's the emergency?"

"Those pricks told me they looked all through the— Fucking idiots." He huffed and motioned to another lackey who'd popped into view, pointing me out. The guy's eyes widened, and he scampered away, presumably to let whoever else was on the lookout that I'd been found. "I wanted to talk to you. About something important."

Important enough that he'd launched a house-wide search. I cocked my head, keeping my own emotions carefully under wraps as if our earlier conversation hadn't happened at all. "Well, I'm here now."

As if on cue, Felix rounded the landing on the staircase

and leaned over the bannister to peer at me. "Ah, there you are, Firebird." He spoke as languidly as he usually did, but he was studying me with unusual intensity.

What the hell had gotten into these guys?

I held out my arms. "Yes, I have arrived. If I'd known I'd become such a celebrity, I wouldn't have waited so long."

He scoffed and turned away, and Darius glowered at… his brother, rather than at me. Okay, something was seriously strange here.

Before I could prompt him to get on with his important talk already, the eldest Rosano brother ushered me over to the staircase, grasping the back of my arm but with more care than when I'd arrived from my trip around the city a couple of hours ago. "Will you come upstairs? I think this should be just between us. We can go to our rooms again—or your room, if you'd rather that."

Between a rock and a hard place. I hated the memories the guys' rooms stirred up, but there'd been plenty of recent encounters in the guestroom that I'd rather not dwell on either. At least the guys' lounge area was larger and didn't contain a literal bed. If I was going to be in close quarters with them, I'd rather it not be *too* close.

"Your rooms are fine," I said briskly, and pulled ahead of him to walk on my own.

When we reached the common room, I stepped to the side of the door, wanting to stay close to it for an easy escape route if I needed one. Darius didn't object. Lucan looked up from where he was sitting at the desk, his hands poised over the keyboard of his laptop, and the same relief

I thought I'd picked up on in Darius's reaction flashed across his face.

He closed the computer and stood up to come around the side of the desk. As he leaned against the edge, crossing his arms over his lean chest, his brothers filled out a semi-circle around me. Darius stayed right in the middle of the room, while Felix sank down on the arm of the sofa. They all fixed their gazes on me as if they were trying to pierce through my skull with their thoughts.

"All right," I said. "Do you want to tell me what the hell is going on, or are you just going to stare at me while I start making random guesses?"

They glanced at each other, and Darius squared his shoulders. "We need to talk about the morning you left."

I frowned at him. "What do you mean? I haven't been out except this evening." Well, and the other night too, but I wasn't going to bring up that stealthy trip even if they already knew about it.

His jaw tightened. "Not now. The last time you were here. After we…"

He trailed off, looking so bizarrely uncertain that suddenly I was pissed off all over again. They'd used me and tossed me aside, and now he was getting all coy about actually saying what we'd done?

"After we all fucked," I said flatly. "When we were teenagers. That's what you're talking about?"

Darius winced, and a flare of the anger that was more his typical expression these days came back into his eyes.

Before he could speak, though, Felix answered me in a drawl. "That would be the thing."

I folded my arms over my chest but refused to give in to the urge to outright hug myself. "What about it?"

"Afterward," Darius said in a growl. "You woke up before us and went out—and you ran into Holly."

I blinked. "She told you that she talked to me?" I wouldn't have thought she'd have admitted to spilling their secrets. And if she had, why were they acting like there was any kind of mystery here? Although maybe she'd only told them that I'd decided to leave and not why.

The edge in Darius's voice sharpened. "Of course she did. Did you really think she wouldn't? We needed to know."

"Well, then, I have no idea what this conversation is supposed to be about," I snapped. "You're already totally filled in, and it obviously didn't make any difference to you."

Darius took a threatening step toward me. "Oh, it made a hell of a lot of difference. To find out you—"

Lucan coughed emphatically, cutting off his brother. "Anthea," he said evenly, "what exactly did you and Holly talk about? Where did you go when you left this room? What were you doing when she found you?"

I dragged in a breath, on the verge of spinning on my heel and stalking out the door without answering. Who the fuck were they to treat this like some kind of interrogation? But the calm in Lucan's voice and the hint of strain underneath it held me in place.

He sounded like he really wanted to know. Like he didn't think he already did.

Even if Holly hadn't told them about our conversation

in full, hadn't they figured out by now that I knew what they'd done?

Fuck it. If they wanted me to rub their faces in it, why the hell not?

"I didn't go anywhere," I said, putting all my concentration into keeping my voice steady. "I was going to wash up and get a change of clothes"—I'd even been thinking I'd whip up a nice breakfast for the guys so we could have a cozy morning together, all giddy after the affection I thought they'd wrapped me up in—"but Holly saw me coming out of your apartment. I guess it wasn't that hard to figure out what'd happened."

Darius had frozen. He stared at me as if I'd said something ridiculous. "She talked to you... right outside the door?" He gestured toward it.

I scowled at him. "Yes. Well, she saw me after a few steps and then motioned me over to the top of the stairs, since she couldn't have known if you'd overhear her. And she told me everything *I* needed to know."

Had Lucan paled? His next question came out even more obviously strained. "And what was that?"

"What do you think? How she'd overheard the three of you joking and making bets with each other on how quickly you could convince me to sleep with you, what you could get me to do with each of you, how you'd decide which of you 'won.'" Acid dripped from my voice. "Maybe whoever managed to fuck me the most before I went home. Maybe if you could convince me to go without protection. Shit like that, laughing the whole time. But she thought it really was just an awful joke until she saw me and realized you'd actually gone through with it, and she was worried that it'd be even worse if she didn't step in then."

Darius's face had gone blotchy, both sallow and flushed. "What?" he said hoarsely. "Why the fuck didn't you say anything to us?"

He really had to ask that?

"What would I have said?" I spat. "'Thanks for having such a good time at my expense, but I'm not actually a sex doll'? I didn't ever want to see you again. I grabbed my stuff and got a cab to the train station. You obviously didn't care that much. You all had my number; you knew where I lived. If you'd been at all concerned, you could have reached out, but I never heard a peep."

As the last words fell from my mouth, I had to stiffen my back to stop myself from sagging. I felt totally drained, even more exhausted than before my basement nap. I did turn then, reaching for the door, but Darius crossed the space between us in a few swift steps and grabbed my arm.

I smacked at him, all patience gone. "Let go of me! You got what you wanted then, and you got me to go over it all again now—you should be perfectly satisfied. Can't you leave me alone for five fucking seconds?"

"No," he said, his voice ragged. "No, we can't. Because that's not what Holly told us, Anthea. And it wasn't— none of it was true."

FIFTEEN

Anthea

MY HEAD JERKED AROUND. I glared at Darius. "What the hell are you talking about? If you really think you can convince me that—"

"Shut up and listen for a second!" he barked, and then shook his head with a pained grimace. "I'm sorry. I'm fucking sorry. I just can't believe— That fucking *cunt.*"

The last few words came out in a snarl, and they obviously weren't directed at me. I hesitated, my arm going limp, and Darius let go of me after all. His fury had sounded totally real.

"What do you mean?" I asked, not liking how small my voice came out sounding but too shellshocked to bolster it.

Felix had shoved himself off the sofa. He stalked over, his mouth twisted. "Holly lied. We never talked about you like that. I sure as hell never *thought* about you like that. Fuck, I'm not exactly Mr. Commitment, but I've never treated *any* woman I've been with or considered being with that horribly."

Lucan had walked closer too, pulling their semi-circle tighter around me. His face had gone totally white, his expression as somber as a funeral.

"We'd talked a little bit about the fact that we were all interested in you," he clarified in his usual factual way. "But never outside our rooms, and never joking about it or making bets or anything creepy like that. All we did was come to the conclusion that we were all attracted to you, and we all wanted to be with you if you were interested, so if you made a move with any of us, then we'd let you pick. At least, that's how it was supposed to work."

He shot a brief glance at Felix, who shrugged and offered a hesitant smirk. "You can't tell a ladies man not to go for it when the vibe is right."

I did remember Lucan saying something about their agreement at the time. My forehead furrowed, a pit opening up in my stomach. "But—why would Holly lie? Why didn't you talk to me after and ask why I'd left?"

"I have no idea why that bitch stuck her nose where it didn't belong and hurled around more shit than a monkey," Darius said, "but she lied to us too. She said she caught you in Dad's office, looking through his files, taking pictures of documents. Spying on the business. That you'd left because she told you to get out—she couldn't let you stay, and she didn't want to find out what we'd do to you if we found out how you'd backstabbed us."

My jaw went slack. "Are you kidding me? Of course I wouldn't have been sneaking around. Why would I be spying on the Hell Kickers? You were our allies. That doesn't even make sense."

Darius threw his hands in the air. "I don't know. Maybe your dad was rethinking the alliance. Maybe your brother had other ideas with his eyes on the inheritance and put you up to it. She sounded convincing, and you *had* left, and we didn't have any reason to think Holly would make up some crazy story. She was arm candy, not some maniacal schemer. At least, as far as we knew."

I absorbed that information, my stomach starting to churn. Holly *had* been quite the schemer, it seemed. I'd known from the comments I'd heard her make to Marcel here and there that she'd imagined herself an ideal partner in his business as well as his personal life, but I hadn't realized she'd taken any kind of covert action on her own.

It'd been such a brilliant scheme that it'd almost lasted forever. She'd pushed just the right buttons to ensure we would never reach out to each other, too horrified by the betrayal—and by how vulnerable we'd gotten right before.

"She knew we'd slept together," I said quietly. "Maybe she'd already figured it out before I came out that morning, and she was waiting for me. She knew it'd have stirred up all kinds of emotions and how easily those could be turned into insecurities. Maniacal isn't even the start of it."

If she'd come to me with claims about the guys saying that kind of crap about me *before* we'd actually acted on the feelings that'd been simmering between us for days— really, for at least a couple of years at that point—I'd have been more confused than wounded. I'd have confronted the guys about it. But hearing it right after I'd let myself get that close to them, done things with them that I'd never done with any other guys, that I'd known my own family would have called me a slut for... It'd been too easy to rattle me, to turn my tentative giddiness into horrifying doubt.

I rubbed my forehead. "I still don't get it. Why would she have wanted to turn us against each other? It's not like I was a threat to her. She never seemed like she minded me coming for those weeks in the summer."

"I don't know," Lucan said. "Maybe she was secretly paranoid, and she thought Dad had been eyeing you and just wanted you out of the house for good."

Felix snorted. "Maybe she was pissed off that she was stuck with his fickle ass and you'd landed not just one but three prime men."

Darius rolled his eyes at his younger brother, but when he glanced back at me, his expression had gone solemn again.

"It doesn't really matter now, does it?" he said. "Whatever it was she was hoping to get, I don't think she did. He divorced her less than a year later. She's out of the picture." He paused. "But we're still in it."

"Yeah." I looked at each of them, the events and emotions of the past few days crashing over me with a dizzying mix of revulsion and regret. "We've been so awful to each other."

"We instigated it," Lucan said with a wince. "We were trying to come down on you hard from the second we found out you'd shown up. If we'd had any idea—"

"You thought you were defending your family," I said. Could I really blame them for that when I'd come here for that exact reason myself? I understood better than they could have realized.

Every vicious moment made perfect sense. I couldn't summon the slightest flicker of anger over it, especially not when the horror at their actions was written so clearly on their faces.

We'd both been fucked over by a woman who was years out of the picture. I'd have liked to punch Holly in her immaculate face given the chance.

Darius growled under his breath. "That isn't an excuse. We *knew* you—we should have realized it couldn't be true. All these fucking years..." He held my gaze, the mix of apology and heat in his eyes making my pulse wobble. "Those years should have been better. They should have been more."

What would my life have been like if their stepmom hadn't destroyed our fledgling romance right after it'd really begun? Would Dad have decided to solidify the alliance between the Nobles and the Hell Kickers by arranging a marriage with one of the brothers after all?

Somehow I couldn't help suspecting he'd still have decided he had more to gain by reeling in Clyde. My preferences had never been a factor, that was for sure.

But now... now we knew. The vibe in the room had changed as the truth had spilled out. I was abruptly, starkly aware that my main reason for holding these guys at arm's length, for teasing our mutual attraction but resisting fully giving in to it, no longer applied.

But only the main reason. And it wasn't even the main reason I'd come.

It seemed my mind wasn't the only one that'd slid in

that direction. Lucan cleared his throat. "Is that why you came here? To get revenge for what you thought we'd done to you?"

At his words, the tentative relief that'd started to soften the tension inside me fell away. My gut sank.

They'd just found out they were wrong about me spying back when I was sixteen. But I *had* come to spy this time.

How could I tell them that? Somehow it'd feel like even more of a betrayal, even though I was more than justified after the crap their people had pulled. I wasn't even totally sure they didn't know about their dad's schemes.

They hadn't been monsters to me seven years ago after all, but I hadn't seen them in all that time. I didn't really know what kind of men they were these days, other than very capable of vengeance when they felt they'd been wronged.

"Maybe a little bit," I said, offering up as much of the truth as I felt I safely could. "My brother did kick me out of our home. I needed to go somewhere. I didn't have a whole lot of options."

Darius's expression had gotten more intense. "You said something when we talked earlier—about us going to war against the Nobles. What was that about?"

Did he really have no idea, or was he testing me to see how *I* knew?

"I've been listening around the house," I admitted, raising my chin as if daring them to take issue with it. "It's obvious everyone here isn't happy about the Nobles. I wanted to make sure I'm actually safe here. I've overheard some things… like your dad and that guy who's hanging around him a lot, Griffin, talking about taking over the Noble-run business here in New York."

Felix snorted as if he thought that idea was absurd.

Lucan's brow furrowed. "I could see them considering the possibility—"

"No," I broke in. "It'd already happened, from what they said." No need to mention that I'd gone out to see for myself, spying on the Hell Kickers outside this house too.

"Bullshit," Darius said. "Dad wouldn't take a step like that without involving us at all."

"Without involving you, you mean," Felix said wryly.

I paused and decided it worked in my favor to reveal one more tidbit. My gaze slid to Darius. "I think Griffin's been trying to get between you and your dad. I heard him saying something about how he'd tried to talk to you about helping with the takeover and you blew him off. But obviously if you didn't even know they were planning it, that was a lie."

Fury flashed in Darius's eyes. "Of course it's a fucking lie. That prick. Who the hell does he think he is?"

Lucan's voice came out quiet but even. "He thinks he's someone who's gotten Dad's ear more than we have it— and it seems like he's right about that. We've just assumed… I didn't realize he'd ingratiated himself so much. Maybe we should have been reaching out to Dad more."

"Fawning over him," Felix said with a hint of a sneer. "We shouldn't need to butter him up. We're *family*. I know I haven't done much for the business, but you and Darius have earned your spots. He shouldn't be shunting you aside over some asshole who puffs up his ego."

"But that doesn't mean he wouldn't," Darius said grimly. "I should have stayed more on top of things. *Fuck.*"

I wavered. They hadn't known about Marcel making plans for war—but did that mean they also had no idea that the deal gone sour had been a setup? They might be hiding that from me just like I was hiding my real purpose here from them.

It didn't seem worth the risk to say anything about my brother's overall innocence. I focused on my own situation instead. "I know your dad sees me as potential leverage—something he might be able to use. I have no idea how this is all going to play out, but you can see why I feel like I'm walking on thin ice in more ways than one."

"Well, first I'll crush that motherfucker," Darius began.

Lucan held up a hand to stop him. "Griffin's been playing a game we weren't aware of. I think we need to determine exactly what his ends are and then undermine him on the same playing field. If we attack him outright without proof that he's done anything wrong, that might just convince Dad that we don't have the family's best interests at heart."

"Fine," Darius grumbled. "But when we do know, I'm looking forward to getting to the crushing part."

He turned to me and took a step forward to set his hand on the side of my arm. With most of my emotional armor against him fallen away, the heat of his touch bloomed all through my body.

"And we'll look after you, Lady Noble," he said, with a promise in his eyes that nearly set me on fire. "Not my dad or Griffin or anyone else is going to lay one finger on you. You've got us watching over you now, like we should have been all along."

Lucan and then Felix nodded in agreement. I offered them a smile of gratitude, my stomach knotting tight.

I still had my own investigation to carry out, and in the blink of an eye, the results could put me at odds with these three men I'd always found so compelling all over again.

SIXTEEN

Lucan

ONCE YOU KNEW the right questions to ask, getting information was often pretty easy. It'd never occurred to me to check whether we were launching a war against the Nobles. But catch a random lackey in the hall and say, "What's the latest on that Noble business we took over?" and a half hour later I found myself getting out of my car outside the office building.

It was obvious both that the takeover had been recent and violent, and that Dad had gotten moving on taking over the place quickly. A few small splatters of blood still marked the front entrance, where Hell Kickers lackeys were ducking in and out. Some of them were sorting through boxes of items that'd been carried into a few of the rooms; others were gabbing away on phones, making arrangements I knew nothing about.

I didn't like it. Slaughtering the Noble people here and claiming the business for ourselves after a decades-long alliance, simply because of a single deal gone wrong? One that Ezra Noble was still claiming he'd fulfilled his end of, pretending we were somehow at fault? If there'd been any hope of sorting out why he'd turned against us, we'd lost it in an instant with this gesture.

He might not have been ready to launch into all-out war, but I doubted he'd believe he had any choice after this.

And where did Anthea fit in, seemingly trapped in the middle of the conflict?

I yanked my thoughts away from her—and her sly smile, and the passion that could burn in her dark gray eyes—to my current target.

"Hey," I said to one of the lackeys. "Where's Griffin at?" I'd gathered from my questions around the house that Dad's new favorite underling had been out here more often than at the brownstone in the last couple of days, overseeing our new operations.

The guy jabbed his thumb toward a room farther back. I stalked down the hallway and found the beefy guy barking orders at a foot soldier who didn't look out of his teens. Apparently he'd put a box in the wrong room or something. I'd have appreciated Griffin being a stickler for details if he wasn't such a dick about it.

As I walked over, the kid scuttled away. Griffin flicked his beady eyes toward me from beneath the messy strands of his reddish-blond hair. I thought I saw him stiffen a little before his expression turned cautious but cold.

"What are you doing here?" he said in a tone that toed the line of being stupidly disrespectful. Something maybe he needed a reminder of.

"I'm checking up on how the transition is going," I said calmly. "Part of the family business; gotta keep an eye on every part of it. I believe in being thorough."

Griffin narrowed his eyes at me. "Marcel said I could take lead here."

Oh, had he? I smiled thinly. "I'm not looking to take over. I've got plenty of other work to take care of. I just like to touch base so I'm aware of what's happening on the ground. My *dad* appreciates the hands-on approach."

I emphasized my connection to the man in charge just in case Griffin needed a firmer reminder of who he was dealing with. The guy's head was obviously getting too big if he was going to argue with one of the Rosano heirs about who had the authority around here.

Griffin simply grunted. I got the impression he wasn't going to volunteer any information—that he'd rather not say anything I didn't drag out of him. Cute.

I glanced around the room. "Things seem pretty busy here already. What all are you setting in motion?"

"Shouldn't you already know all about that, since it's your business?" Griffin said, dodging the question and aiming another jab at the same time.

I fixed my gaze on him again and folded my arms over my chest. "I'm asking what *you* have managed to establish here so far. Seeing as you're taking lead and all. Or do you not know what you're leading?"

My own jab landed. The guy's face flushed with a ruddy hue I suspected was both embarrassment and fury over the fact that I'd made him feel embarrassed.

"The Nobles had a gambling operation running out of here, among other things," he said tightly. "We're picking up as many threads as we can to get that up and running again. There's a bunch of goods they were hiding behind the shoe store front that we claimed and are sorting through. And I'm still deciding whether we'll keep the store as is or present something different as the legitimate front that'll work to launder proceeds as well. Does that meet your satisfaction?"

Not really. He was still being fairly vague about his plans. I was surer than ever that he didn't want me knowing anything more about what he was up to than he had to share.

It didn't sound as if he was setting up anything particularly controversial here, though. That made sense. He wouldn't want to go too big or risky on the first project he'd been put in charge of. He wanted to impress Dad, sure, but to be certain he'd pull it off as well.

"It was a bold move, grabbing this property from the Nobles," I said conversationally, not letting any hint of my opinion color my voice.

Griffin let out a huff. "They deserved us coming down on them hard after how they screwed us over. It was ridiculous that we waited even this long to make a move." His mouth pressed flat for a second as if he realized he'd said more than was wise, and then he added quickly, "Marcel agrees. He couldn't stand back any longer."

"Right," I said dryly. No doubt because this prick had gotten in Dad's ear and incited him to act. Who knew what lies he'd made up if he'd been telling stories about Darius?

The trouble was, if the bastard had already infected Dad's mind against us, we wouldn't get straight answers out of our own father either. I resisted the urge to grit my teeth.

"I suppose you have big plans for working Ezra Noble's sister for information too, then," I went on. "Dad came up with a good gambit, taking advantage of her distress and getting her into the home where we can control her."

After hearing from Darius how Anthea had been controlled before, the abuse she'd faced, the words tasted bitter in my mouth, but I needed Griffin to think I was on his side.

The guy shrugged. "We're still working out the best approach," he said, hedging again. And I couldn't miss the familiarity in that "we," as if he and Dad were some kind of decisive unit.

"As long as everyone who needs to be in the know is kept in the loop," I said evenly.

Griffin jutted his chin at a haughty angle. "Oh, Marcel knows who he can count on."

I shot him a brief glower. "I'm sure he does."

But the remark rang in my mind as I headed out of the office building. A certainty twisted around my gut, uncomfortably tight.

Griffin was definitely aiming to make himself the man Dad counted on most—and it looked like he was succeeding. We'd gotten too complacent, too used to the roles we'd started to take for granted—it'd never occurred to me that someone might weasel in there so effectively that Dad would end up cutting us out.

That was what this prick intended, though. I had no

doubt. He wanted to be next in line for the throne. Fucking hell.

There might be an easy solution to that problem. Griffin was obviously leveraging the conflict with the Nobles to major effect. Which meant it was possible he'd been instrumental in making that conflict occur. It was time I had a talk with our man who'd been on the ground during the deal gone wrong, who'd I'd sent into that fray inadvertently, and find out if anyone on our own side might have interfered.

Dad wouldn't let some asshole who'd undermined his own operations walk away alive.

I found Mick out at one of our main warehouses, where he spent most of his time when he wasn't discussing operations with me or Dad or overseeing a deal in progress. He was consulting with one of the warehouse workers with a much calmer disposition than I'd seen from Griffin. But then, I'd always thought Mick was one of our most reliable lieutenants. He'd been around since I was a kid, and he made a point of always delivering what was asked of him.

The deaths from a couple weeks ago had to be eating at him. It was the first time any deal he'd been managing directly had gone anywhere near that sour.

Also in stark contrast to the leech, Mick gave me a nod of deferential acknowledgment when he saw me. *He* recognized my position in the Hell Kickers.

"Lucan," he said in his low voice. "What can I help you with? Is there a concern with the numbers from the recent shipments?"

That was the sort of thing I'd normally have dropped

by to ask him about. I shook my head and motioned him over to the far end of the warehouse, away from the underlings at work.

"I'm sorry to bring this up after I'm sure you'd hashed it out more times than you'd have liked to already," I said, "but I need to ask you something about the recent exchange with the Nobles—the one that ended with the shootout."

Mick's expression tightened, but he inclined his head. "Of course. If I can help make something good come out of that mess, or at least make it less bad, I'm all for it."

He really was a decent man. I offered him a warmer smile than I'd given Griffin. "You might have noticed that my dad has been consulting with a guy named Griffin quite a bit. Have you talked to him at all?"

"Griffin…" Mick seemed to test the name out. "Big guy, light hair, kind of squinty?"

My lips twitched with suppressed amusement at the description. "That would be the one."

"I've seen him around. What about him?"

"I was just wondering if he was at all involved in the deal or the arrangements for the hand-off. Passing information between you and other parties, scoping out possible sites, that kind of thing."

Mick frowned. "I don't think I talked to him at all while we were putting that in motion. As far as I know, he had no idea it was even going down. It wasn't a particularly significant deal until it went wrong, you know. On the larger side, but not out of the norm. It should have been business as usual."

"Yeah." My stomach knotted. "Has he mentioned anything to you about it since then?"

"Not directly. I heard him saying some aggressive stuff about how the Nobles should pay to some of the younger guys once, but I couldn't say I disagree with him."

"They're definitely going to regret screwing us over," I said. If they didn't already. It didn't sound as if Mick was going to help me put any more of the pieces together, though. I dipped my head to him. "Thanks for talking with me."

"Any time. You know I'm with the Hell Kickers to the end."

I was ruminating over what I'd seen and heard so deeply as I returned home that I almost didn't notice Anthea coming down the hall from her room as I passed by. Almost. That bright red hair drew my attention like a flame, jerking me out of my reverie.

I stopped at the base of the stairs to the third floor, letting her come to me. Watching her graceful strides, desire unfurled through my belly, enough to make my cock twitch. Partly because I couldn't look at her without remembering how she'd felt under me on her bed the other night.

I'd already made a fool of myself then. I wasn't going to again. Besides, I wasn't completely convinced that Anthea was a victim *now*, even if she had been before. Something didn't feel quite right about her sudden arrival here, no matter what stories she gave us.

Somehow or other, I'd get to the bottom of that problem too.

Offering her a little information could be one way to

ferret out more from her. I beckoned her a little closer, bracing myself against the deeper flare of attraction that rose up when she was standing only a few feet away.

"I've been making the rounds," I said quietly. "Chatted up Griffin and our guy who made it out of the shootout with the Nobles alive, Mick."

Her eyes lit up with interest. "Did they have anything interesting to say?"

I couldn't read anything specific into that question. Of course she'd want to know.

I grimaced. "We definitely need to put Griffin back in his place. But from what Mick said, the guy is only taking advantage of the new animosity toward the Nobles. He didn't incite the trouble. It sounds like he probably wouldn't have realized that deal was even happening to interfere with it."

Anthea hummed to herself, a faint furrow forming in her brow. She studied me. "Did Mick seem to mind you asking about the deal?" she asked.

Why would she think he might? Or had she just heard about his frustration over the losses? It was a little odd that she'd be concerned about a guy she barely knew, though.

I shook my head, keeping my confusion to myself. "Not at all. I know he's torn up about what happened, but he's always kept it professional. He'd do whatever he can to help us recover."

Her eyebrows rose slightly. "You trust him a lot."

"Sure. He's been with the family for ages. Never hesitated in the line of duty." I gave a light laugh. "And Dad started giving him a cut of every deal he handles, so he's making a good living out of us too."

I couldn't tell what Anthea made of that information, but she didn't look totally happy about it. "Why are you asking?" I added abruptly.

She waved her hand dismissively, her fingertips grazing my arm for just long enough to set off fresh sparks. "Oh, I just thought I should make sure, since he is so involved. This Griffin guy seems like the bigger problem."

Yes, he was. But I still wasn't completely convinced that the woman in front of me wasn't the biggest problem of all.

SEVENTEEN

Anthea

I DIDN'T LIKE UNCERTAINTY. I worked best with facts and charts, scientific data on chemical interactions, concrete methodologies—knowing the precise increments that made the difference between success and failure, life and death. Freedom and imprisonment. So Lucan's claim about Mick's loyalty gnawed at me all through the day.

He should know the man a lot better than I did. Of course, it wouldn't be the first time a supposedly loyal underling had betrayed his boss. People got away with that sort of thing precisely because they were good at hiding their intentions.

Really, it was Lucan's comment about Mick getting a cut from the business that caused me the most concern. Money troubles were the best motivation I'd been able to come up with for Mick to orchestrate the failed deal. Unless he'd gotten very careless with his cash and racked up some major gambling debts or made some incredibly bad investments that meant he needed a ton of money immediately, sticking with Marcel and picking up a percentage of profits should have been his best bet financially.

On the other hand, could I believe he was *so* loyal to Marcel that he'd been willing to kill his own men, whose deaths everyone I'd spoken to about him had agreed he seemed torn up about, simply because his boss asked him to so that they could spark a war? I hadn't gotten the impression that Mick had any reason to hold a grudge against the Nobles before that incident.

Desperation could make men turn to violence against their principles; loyalty was harder to leverage that way. If he was a good man, he'd have felt a duty to protect the lackeys working under him too.

There was way too much I still didn't know. I hadn't even determined whether Marcel or Griffin or both had been in on the sabotaged deal or were simply exploiting an unexpected turn of events.

The Rosano brothers didn't know everything that was going on between their father and the lower echelons of the Hell Kickers. Maybe Marcel had revoked his deal with Mick. Maybe there'd been some other conflict between them. Hell, for all I knew, Griffin had seen the guy as a threat to his rise and sabotaged him in some way.

I needed more information.

I didn't expect to get anything out of Marcel or Mick directly, but when I spotted Brant in the kitchen turning the coffee maker on, I glommed on to the opportunity to at least get pointed in the direction of solid evidence. The curly-haired guy wasn't exactly friendly, but he seemed to get around in the business. And he worked in a similar line to Mick's.

I grabbed a mug of my own out of the cupboard as if I'd been coming in here for that purpose anyway and sidled over to the stocky man. "Put in enough for me too?"

He grunted. "I always make a full pot. Common courtesy."

He'd left a small canvas shoulder bag on one of the chairs by the kitchen island. I leaned against the counter next to it, glancing it over, and took inspiration for a conversation opener. "If I had a few more items I wanted to fence, just to get my cash flow up to speed, you'd be able to handle that for me again?"

"I could probably fit it in. What've you got this time?"

"I'm not sure yet if I want to give them up… Just good to know I have the option. I ended up talking to Mick a little while ago, since you said moving goods is his specialty, but it seemed like he's focused on bigger things."

"He's a big shot, all right," Brant muttered.

I thought I detected a hint of animosity in the words. "I guess he must work very closely with Marcel. Special projects and all that."

"I don't know anything about it," Brant said, even gruffer than before. "He's too busy to train me up into his operations." His mouth flattened, and he shook his head. "I don't need anything from him anyway. Just doesn't feel much like a team effort."

Mick was being kind of secretive about how he ran things, then. That was interesting. Maybe I should find a lackey or two who'd supported him in other deals. He might not want to bring Brant on board as a potential second-in-command, but he needed grunt workers, and they often saw things the higher-ups didn't realize.

The coffee maker burbled, the dark liquid rising almost to the top of the glass pot. Brant jerked it out, sloshed some in his mug, and turned to go. As an excuse to get a feel for what might be inside it, because you never knew what details might be useful later, I snatched up his bag and handed it to him.

My fingers closed around what felt like an ordinary wallet through the canvas, the light bag not holding much else. But as it moved through the air, a whiff of a faintly floral scent tickled my nose, like a woman's perfume.

Apparently some gal found this guy appealing enough to hang around him. There was no accounting for gang groupie tastes.

Brant yanked the bag away from me and strode out of the room. The coffee smelled unappealingly bitter, but the caffeine would give me a boost of alertness. I poured myself half a cup and sipped it while I put together a quick lunch from the offerings in the fridge. While a few other Hell Kickers underlings wandered in and out, I made myself inobtrusive, standing off in the corner. None of their conversations gave me any enlightenment, though.

I was heading back to my room, frustration gnawing at me, when Felix caught me on the stairs. He grinned at me, all trace of the hostility that'd colored our interactions for the past few days vanished, and damn it, my heart skipped a beat. I'd always found his combination of dark hair and bright eyes irresistible when he brought out his playfully carefree attitude. It'd never seemed like the weight of his position in the world got him down—until recently.

And now he knew that I wasn't a scheming traitor—or at least, I hadn't been at sixteen—and the clouds had parted. He tapped my arm, his gaze turning sly. "Come upstairs, Firebird. I've got something important to tell you."

Another giddy jolt shot through me, this one because it was possible he'd offer a morsel that'd bring everything I'd learned together into a more coherent picture. I followed him up to the third floor, allowing myself the indulgence of admiring his toned ass now that I knew *he* hadn't been an asshole all those years ago either.

The brothers' common room was empty when we stepped inside. Felix motioned me in all gentleman-like, closed the door behind us—and then pushed me up against the wall next to it as if being a gentleman was the last thing on his mind.

His muscular body aligned with mine, flooding me with heat. One hand came to rest on my hip, the other delving into my hair. He smirked at me, his gorgeous face just inches away. My breath caught in my throat.

"You said you wanted to tell me something," I pointed out, managing to keep my voice reasonably steady even though all my nerves were quivering in anticipation. "This seems like a strange way to have a conversation."

"I don't know," Felix said in a wry tone. He lowered his head, letting his lips brush the side of my neck. "I think all the best conversations happen with a woman pinned against a wall."

I snorted but didn't quite manage to restrain a gasp as

he nicked his teeth against the perfect spot at the crook of my shoulder. The heat generated between our bodies was pooling between my thighs.

There'd been so much teasing between me and all three of the Rosano brothers over the past few days that I was dying for a proper release. Even if I wasn't totally sure how far I could trust them when it came to business, it wouldn't be so unwise to allow for a little personal time with them, would it?

My pride wouldn't let me give in quite that easily, though. I ran my fingers into Felix's floppy hair, reveling in the silky texture, and gripped hard in a reminder that I wasn't any shrinking wallflower. "And what exactly was it you wanted to talk about?"

"Isn't it obvious? I thought you were sharper than that, Firebird." Felix trailed his lips up the side of my neck and nibbled my earlobe. At the flick of his tongue, a bolt of pleasure quivered through me. I clamped my mouth shut against a whimper.

"I think we should finish what we started in the coat closet," he went on in a husky murmur. "In a way I'm sure we'll both find much more satisfying." The hand on my hip slipped between us, cupping me through my dress.

My chest hitched, my eyes rolling upward as Felix caressed my clit, gently and then more firmly until I couldn't hold back a ragged exhalation.

Oh, fuck, yes. His erection pressed against my thigh, straining at the fly of his jeans. It was probably only fair if I repaid the favor.

"Are you that desperate for a hand job?" I had to tease,

shifting my weight so that my hip rubbed against his groin.

Felix let out a pleased growl and dropped his hand. The sense of loss jolted through me for just a moment before he was hiking up my skirt and tucking his fingers right against my panties. He hooked a finger around the dampening fabric and tugged it to the side to stroke my folds skin to skin.

Pleasure surged up through my abdomen, and this time a whimper tumbled out before I could catch it. My body arched toward him instinctively.

The youngest Rosano brother leaned in close, his nose grazing my cheek. "I expect it'll lead to a lot more than hands," he said. "Your brother screwed over both of us, but we can make some good screwing out of the aftermath, huh?"

Then his mouth captured mine before I could say anything at all in response. His finger curled right inside me, and I moaned against his lips.

Felix took the opportunity to delve his tongue into my mouth, tangling with mine. I kissed him back hard, bliss searing all through my body as he plundered me above and below. But even as the heady pleasure of his touch consumed me, his words stuck in my mind.

He'd made the comment without artifice or anything to gain. I was pretty sure he meant it. He believed that Ezra had screwed over his family, not the other way around.

And if he was sure of that, then I could be pretty much certain Darius and Lucan weren't in on the double-cross either. They were as tightly entwined as they'd always been. I couldn't see them keeping information that vital from each other.

Which meant I could give myself over to this moment without the slightest bit of guilt that I might be consorting with the enemy.

I wasn't giving much back yet. I nipped Felix's lower lip, making him hiss and claim my mouth with even more force, and reached for his fly with my free hand. No point in bothering with fumbling through layers of fabric; I was going straight for the prize.

As I tugged the zipper down, Felix stroked a second finger into my slit. His thumb flicked back and forth over the pulsing nub just above it, and I clutched his hair even tighter. Fucking hell, he did know what he was doing. Imagine how good it could be once we got past just hands.

I shoved my fingers right into his boxers and wrapped them around his rigid cock. Felix groaned, bucking into my grasp. As I started to pump him, slicking his precum down his length, he released my mouth to chart a scorching path along my jaw.

"So fucking good," he muttered against my skin, his fingers still thrusting inside me, reaching deeper with each giddy press of my clit. "Even when I thought *you'd* screwed us over, I kept coming back to that night, getting off on the thought of you."

He'd fantasized about our group hook-up that much? It'd sounded like he'd gotten around with plenty of other women both before and after.

I sucked in an uneven breath around a fresh jolt of pleasure and released a faint laugh. "It was so special, was it?"

Felix hesitated, his breath washing over my neck, his fingers slowing inside me to the point that I almost groaned in protest. Then he worked them faster again, swiveling his thumb and giving my jaw a little love bite.

"*You're* special," he said, so quietly I wasn't totally sure he wanted me to hear him. "You always were. There's never been any other woman I've wanted the way I want you—not just to get off but… everything."

My throat choked up at the strained emotion in his voice. "Everything?" I murmured.

"Everything you'll fucking give me," he said with a ragged chuckle, and melded his mouth to mine.

I didn't know how to answer his confession, didn't know how to react to the way it lit me up inside. I'd thought the weird connection I'd felt with the brothers I'd spent weeks of my summer with for years had been mostly on *my* end, because I hadn't had much chance to crush on anyone else. But maybe it had been special in a general sense. I'd never been drawn to any of the many guys around the Noble mansion in the same way.

Something about the Rosano brothers had called to me from the start. The idea that it'd been the same for them, or at least for Felix, was both reassuring and electrifying.

I kissed him back with everything I had in me, as if I could tell him I wanted the same thing without using any words. My hand jerked up and down around his cock, my thumb tracing the underside and swiveling over the head so that he let out another groan.

He added a third finger inside me, stretching me with a delicious burn that had me gasping and pumping him even harder. Our hips swayed in the same rhythm, our panted breaths mingling.

Felix swiped hard across my clit in time with a plunge of his fingers that hit my G-spot, and my vision whited out with the burst of ecstasy. I cried out into his mouth, both my hand and my pussy clenching around him, and he came with me in a hot spurt across my wrist.

"Fuck," he said roughly, his head bowing next to mine as he leaned into me. "I didn't mean to—but feeling you get there—" He drew back a little to meet my eyes, a spark of mischief lighting in his. "Give me a few minutes, and I'll be up and raring to go again. We're definitely not—"

The door beside us thumped open. "If you think about it," Darius was just saying to Lucan as they strode inside, and then he cut himself off, both of them stalling in their tracks as they stared at Felix and me.

Darius's shoulders stiffened, his next words coming out just shy of a roar. "What the fuck is going on here?"

EIGHTEEN

Anthea

I JERKED my hand from inside Felix's jeans, starkly aware of the cooling wetness of his cum splattered across my forearm. The youngest Rosano brother proved himself to be something of a gentleman after all by catching my fingers and wiping off the mess on his own shirt rather than leaving me to deal with it myself. Not that there would be any doubt about what had just happened between us.

Which made Darius's question particularly absurd.

As Felix yanked himself back into his jeans and the skirt of my dress fell back to my knees, I narrowed my eyes at the other two brothers. Darius was glaring at both of us, fuming so visibly I was surprised smoke wasn't pouring off the top of his head. Lucan's mouth had gone deathly tight.

For fuck's sake. "What does it look like's going on here?" I shot back. "Never had a good enough time with the groupies to figure it out?"

Darius's lips drew back in what could only be considered a snarl, though it was directed more at Felix than at me. "Jumping in there the first instant you could just like last time."

Felix held up his hands in a gesture of surrender, his cocky smile gone a bit shaky around the edges. They might be brothers, but he knew who laid down the law between the three of them. "It worked out well before."

"And you never thought—"

"Whoa!" I said, stepping between them and giving both of them a push in opposite directions. Felix stepped back at my touch, but Darius didn't budge. "What are you so angry about? I thought we cleared the air here, no more seeing me as the enemy. Why the hell shouldn't I hook up with Felix if I want to?"

"He knows we all— We haven't had a chance to decide —" Darius gave a growl of frustration. He loomed over Felix despite my attempt at intervening and swiped his arm through the air. "Get out."

Lucan spoke up, his voice tersely even. "Darius, maybe we should—"

"You too," Darius said, spinning around. "Both of you, now. Find something actually useful to do with yourselves."

Felix's mouth twisted. He stalked past Darius out of the room. Lucan gave the two of us an uncertain look, but when Darius aimed his glare at his brother, he left too. The door thudded shut in their wake.

Darius rounded on me.

"What the fuck are you doing?" I demanded before he could speak.

"What the fuck are *you* doing?" he retorted, stepping closer. I dodged to the side before he could get me up against the wall like his brother had. "We only just sorted things out, and you're already flinging yourself into *Felix's* arms?"

I scowled at him, folding my arms over my chest. "Why shouldn't I? We *did* sort things out. All's well, right? Or am I somehow still not good enough for anyone in the family? Tainted by whatever my brother's done or some shit like that?"

Darius let out a huff. "Of course you're good enough. But Felix… Yes, he's family, but haven't you seen how he is? He humps every female-shaped thing that walks through his view."

"Then he should know what he's doing," I said tartly. "Sounds like a plus to me."

"He shouldn't be doing it with *you*. You deserve better than a quick fuck against the wall, or I'd have— After what you went through with that asshole your dad sent you off to—"

The pieces were starting to click in my head. I raised my chin. "Ah. I think I'm seeing the problem. It's not that I was having fun with Felix. It's that for some stupid reason, you thought you had first dibs. I'm sure your brother would love to know you think so highly of him."

Darius's eyes flashed. "That's not the point."

"I think it is. And you know what, your little brother was a hell of a lot sweeter to me just now than you've been even since you found out the truth. I don't think he was planning on tossing me aside after a quick pump-and-dump."

Darius clenched his hands at his sides, and I got the abrupt impression that the idea of Felix staking a more permanent claim bothered him even more. "What did he say?"

I glowered at him. "That's none of your business."

"I say what's my business. Tell me what he said."

"You might be able to order your brothers around, but you don't have any authority over me."

With a ragged exhalation, Darius lunged forward. He moved too suddenly and quickly for me to flee. He scooped up my much smaller frame, shoved past the door to his bedroom, and heaved me down on the edge of the bed, setting his hands on my shoulders to hold me in place.

I braced my hands against the covers, shooting murder at him with my eyes, but a tremor I couldn't control ran through my body. Remembering Clyde's weight pressing me down, the cutting edge of his voice with his constant demands. My fingers dug into the blanket.

"For someone who talks like he's so concerned about my late husband, you're sure doing a great job of imitating him."

Darius flinched. He ripped his hands away from me, taking a step back. The color drained from his face as he stared back at me. He opened his mouth and closed it again as if he couldn't quite find his words.

"Sorry," he said finally, hoarsely. "I didn't—*fuck*."

To my shock, he lowered himself onto his knees in front of me, the humble pose putting us at eye level. He took my hand from my lap—carefully, as if to make sure I wouldn't jerk it away from him. He looked at it and then at me, so many emotions roiling through his cool blue eyes that I couldn't look away.

"I'm sorry," he said again. "I've been a prick since you got here, and I'm only making it worse. This isn't how I wanted to do this. I just—I saw you with Felix—something snapped in my head. But I wouldn't hurt you. I'd never be like that fucker you had to marry."

My own anger simmered down. "Then what's with all the yelling and the carrying me around?" I asked in a quieter voice.

Darius rubbed his forehead. "I thought if I could get you in here and we could just talk it out, if I could find the right way to tell you..."

"Tell me what?" I prompted when he fell silent. It seemed like the whole clamming up thing was spreading through the Rosano brothers like a plague.

He looked up at me, squeezing my hand. "I've tried to protect my brothers from dealing with a lot of the shit that comes with ruling a family like ours. I came down on you when you showed up thinking I was protecting them from *you*. But you were the one who needed protection—you *have* needed it, all this time, while I was hating you and hating myself for missing the signs that you'd turned on us."

I gripped his fingers in return. "I didn't expect you to protect me, Darius."

"I know. But I want to. There's always been something about you... so fucking strong and fierce in that little body... I wanted you back then, and I want you now. If we could start over, do this right—you wouldn't need to worry about anything. I won't let my dad or your brother or any other prick fuck up your life ever again."

A lump rose in my throat like it had at Felix's declaration. I leaned forward and grazed my other hand over Darius's short hair. He tipped into my touch, his gaze darkening with desire so potent it tingled over my skin.

"What if I feel the same way I did back then?" I asked. "What if I don't know how to pick between the three of you? Maybe it's selfish, but… I spent five years suppressing everything I wanted to cater to the men who thought they owned me. I don't want to be trapped like that again. If I'm going to be with anyone, it's got to be without any chains."

Darius swallowed audibly. He stroked his free hand up and down my bare calf, and damn if my panties didn't start to melt all over again. "I don't know if I can stand by and watch you take up with every guy you like the look of. It killed me seeing you with Felix, thinking I'd lost my chance."

"I'm not saying I want to fuck every guy who crosses my path. But the four of us made it work that one night seven years ago, didn't we? Could you stand it if it was just your brothers? For now, anyway, while I'm figuring things out?" My lips twitched with a smile. "I think between the three of you, you'll keep me too busy for me to even think about anyone else." I'd never wanted anyone else anyway, but I wasn't sure I was ready to admit that.

Darius paused. Then his hand slid a little higher, over my knee. To my relief, he offered a small smile in response. "I bet we would. Maybe I should get started on that right now, just to make sure those pretty eyes of yours don't go wandering any farther."

Before I could answer, he lowered his head to kiss the side of my knee. As my fingers curled against his scalp, he eased the skirt of my dress up in the wake of the path he was marking with his lips. His mouth seared my skin, edging closer to the aching core of me until I had to splay my legs farther apart.

Was this a good idea? I didn't know. But it felt too good for me to come up with any arguments for stopping.

Darius pushed my skirt all the way up to my waist and grasped my panties. As he pulled them off, torturously slowly, an eager shiver raced through me.

"No biting?" I had to ask. "I hope you don't have payback in mind."

Darius chuckled, nothing but lust shining in his eyes now. "I fucking deserved that. You could have bitten me a lot harder, and I probably still would have. But you can consider this payback for all the times in the past week that I've come picturing you writhing and moaning under me."

Then he pushed his face between my legs and swiped his tongue right over me.

I gave a little cry just at that first rush of sensation. Darius didn't hesitate but got right down to devouring me. He might not have been planning to chomp on my delicate bits the way I had to him, but he brought the tips of his teeth to bear alongside his lips and tongue. They scraped over my clit, sending a spike of pleasure through me that surged even higher when he sucked down hard.

"Fuck," I muttered, clutching the back of his head with one hand and the covers with the other.

As he lapped his tongue in and out of me, I rocked my hips to meet his thrusts. I'd just come harder than I had in years with Felix, and now an even hotter explosion was building inside me, expanding from my pussy through my body by the second.

Darius plunged two fingers into me while slicking his tongue back and forth over my clit. He pumped them in and out with practiced assurance I didn't want to think too much about, stroking the perfect spot inside me.

His teeth grazed my clit again, followed by a more emphatic sucking. His other hand squeezed my ass. I moaned and bucked to meet him, and he hit me at just the right spot inside to send me soaring.

I careened on a wave of bliss and sank down through the heated afterglow as if gliding on a cloud. Darius didn't let up. He eased up his pace only for an instant and then started working me over as emphatically as before.

Yet another knot of ecstasy swelled in my core. His curled fingers stroked against my G-spot, and his tongue circled my clit. He propelled me over the edge a second time in less than a minute, leaving me gasping and twice as boneless as before.

Darius nuzzled my pussy to provoke a few final sparks of pleasure and then grinned up at me, not just lust but undeniable affection warming his gaze.

Matching affection washed through me. I held out my hand to him. "Come here. And please tell me you have a good supply of condoms."

A laugh burst out of him. He climbed onto the bed

next to me and pulled me into a scorching embrace, but he didn't make any move to strip his own clothes off.

"I think we'll leave it there for now," he said. "Because I'm not like the asshole you were married to, and I don't want you to ever think otherwise. I can give without taking anything."

I swallowed thickly and peered at him through my eyelashes. What was I even doing? How could this go anywhere when I still had my mission here to see through?

They had to understand. They had to see that defending my family mattered just as much to me as defending theirs did to them, and that someone in the Hell Kickers had done us wrong.

"Even though I'm a treacherous Noble," I said lightly but only partly joking.

Darius scoffed. "You're not part of your brother's plans. The Hell Kickers' blood that was spilled is on his hands, not yours."

I was a much bigger part of those plans than he knew, but not in the way he'd have thought. I couldn't help pointing out, just to prod the subject a little farther along: "There was blood spilled on the Nobles side too, you know."

"Of course. Once someone starts shooting, we're going to shoot back. Are you going to hold that against us?"

He blew teasingly into my hair, but my eyes had popped open wider as the full implications of his words hit me.

He was right. Once *someone* started shooting, the people being shot back would retaliate.

But what if the first shooter hadn't been on either side but somewhere else altogether?

NINETEEN

Anthea

THE SITE of the deal-gone-wrong was less ominous by the late afternoon light. The warehouses looked even more derelict when I could make out the cracks in the windowpanes and the crumbling bricks in greater detail. The lot's dusty asphalt didn't impress either.

I stalked along the same course I'd taken the first night, no faster for the increased visibility. Any tiny detail could tell the story I was hoping to uncover.

The markings in the walls where stray bullets had hit the bricks lined up with the spots where I believed each gang had been staked out... except for that one that looked oddly wide. And after several minutes of careful searching, I spotted a bit of shell casing on the asphalt much farther away in the opposite direction, off to the side, several meters from where the shipping crate now stood. A spot where I could make out a few even fainter scuff marks on the asphalt that suggested this was where it'd been shoved from afterward to make its usefulness as cover for a sniper less obvious.

I didn't find any other evidence right there, but when I scanned the warehouses' walls with that spot in mind, I caught sight of another bullet lodged in the bricks several meters farther from the shootout, where no one on either side would have had any business aiming. But someone firing into the fray from a more distant angle? They could have lodged one there.

Certainty gripped my gut alongside an unexpected surge of relief. No matter what had happened since then, *neither* gang had betrayed the other in the deal. Both the Nobles and the Hell Kickers had been incited into action by a totally separate shooter. Whoever it'd been had probably fired at each side right after the other so both had seen a man fall and assumed the other gang had been responsible.

Why wouldn't they have? It'd been too dark to easily make out where the first shots had come from, especially when they'd have been out of the blue, taking the groups by surprise. And then they'd have been too caught up in defending themselves to talk things out.

The sniper could have crouched down behind the shipping crate while the rest of the carnage played out, fired off a few more shots at the end to drive the survivors away from the goods, and then grabbed the money and the truck and taken off with them. Leaving both sides to blame the other.

I'd bet later that night the mysterious shooter had returned to clean up as much of the evidence as possible, but it was difficult to catch everything. They wouldn't have wanted to linger at the scene.

Why would someone have wanted to screw over both the Nobles and the Hell Kickers? That was the big question. I hadn't heard about any other recent, significant conflicts between Ezra and another syndicate. None of the Hell Kickers had mentioned other enemies they were keeping an eye on.

I'd ask around just to be sure, but my gut already told me that this wasn't a typical business move. It was personal.

I walked back to the area where it looked like the shipping crate had once stood, and a suspicion tickled at the back of my mind. The shooter's stakeout spot had been clos*er* before, but still quite a distance from the part of the lot where the gang men had parked, far enough that no one would have scoped it out. The gunman had wanted to be sure he'd have a clear aim at both sides without them noticing him. To hit the necessary targets in the dark would have required someone who was quite a good shot.

I couldn't help remembering the night I'd wandered into the basement and seen a bunch of the Hell Kickers underlings goofing around with Nerf guns. How I'd watched Brant fudge his shots and then show off his perfect aim when he thought no one was watching.

He happened to have connections when it came to fencing stolen goods too. And he'd acted cagey when I'd asked him about Mick, the sole remaining survivor of that shootout on the Hell Kickers' side.

The proof was all circumstantial at this point, but Brant was the only person close to the conflict I'd observed who seemed like a viable suspect. Griffin had motive if he'd wanted to push his agenda against the Nobles and maybe pick off a few other key underlings he might have seen as competition, but it wasn't clear he'd had any idea the deal was even taking place, and he didn't seem concerned that anyone might suspect him of turning on his own people. Mick must have been with his men, or they wouldn't have continued with the deal.

Possibly some other player had sent a shooter in, but from what I'd seen, the simplest explanation was usually the correct one. There was no point in looking for other suspects farther abroad when I had one right in front of me.

Even if Brant had launched the attack, I still didn't know why. Had it been an effort at undermining Mick, since he seemed to resent the older man for not taking him more under his wing? Pure greed, wanting to make some extra cash on the side and not caring who he hurt? I didn't know what he'd have against the Nobles, but he might have seen them as a convenient red herring rather than having a personal vendetta against both sides.

I headed back to the Rosanos' brownstone but didn't go inside. Instead, I waited in the lengthening evening shadows down the street, watching the comings and goings. Brant was often around during the day, and I'd seen him in the hall shortly before I left, but I didn't think he normally stayed overnight.

Around eight, I spotted his stocky form heading out the front door. I gripped my phone in case I needed to quickly hail an Uber, but he set off on foot. The lackeys frequently did, Brooklyn being pretty walkable and the traffic often wretched.

I followed him at a discreet distance, walking swiftly but quietly and keeping close to the buildings. He strode along quickly, not glancing back, the messenger bag he'd had with him earlier slung over his shoulder. A couple of times, he made sudden detours as if he was trying to ensure no one would be able to stay on his trail, but I didn't let him shake me. The brief attempts at subterfuge only intensified my suspicions.

We left behind the residential streets for a commercial strip, passed some apartment buildings, and entered another shopping area. Finally, Brant ducked through the doorway of a café, its sidewalk patio closed for the evening but the lights gleaming inside.

I slunk to the edge of the glow and peered inside.

Brant was just sitting down at a small table at the back of the space, across from a slim woman with a pale pixie cut. Well, I had figured he was seeing someone, although I hadn't realized it was more serious than some hookups with a gang groupie. Was this just a dinner date?

But something about the woman's face held my attention. I squinted at her, taking in her profile, the flicker of her tight smile, and the way she tugged at the short strands of blond hair at the back of her neck. Then she glanced toward the front of the café, giving me a full-face view, and my body stiffened.

It was Holly—Marcel's ex-wife, the Rosano brothers' former stepmother. The woman who'd lied to me about them making bets on how they could use me while fibbing to them about my supposed spying around the house. She'd cut her hair shorter, but it was the same icy shade, and her features were only a little more lined with age than they'd been seven years ago. She'd been pretty young back then—she couldn't be older than her late thirties even now.

What the hell was Brant doing with *her*? From what the guys had said, Marcel had divorced her not long after the last time I'd seen her. She didn't have any business with his family or the Hell Kickers anymore, not that she'd ever been part of the gang in the first place.

As much as she'd tried to get her husband to let her in on his business endeavors…

Understanding unfurled in my head. Hell hath no fury like a woman scorned, right? I should know something about that. How pissed off might she have been when Marcel ended things and moved on to a younger model? And she'd obviously disliked me for whatever reasons, so maybe she'd liked the idea of sticking it to my family at the same time.

She'd weaseled her way back into Marcel's business through the back door, found herself an inside man as her accomplice, and undermined one of his longest-standing alliances. What else did she have planned for the Rosanos while Brant could give her the inside scoop?

This… was not at all what Ezra had been expecting when he'd sent me here. He'd thought I could find the culprits right within the Hell Kickers' ranks and deal out vengeance there. Holly was a wild card neither of us would have anticipated.

I could still get our vengeance, but I didn't know how quickly I could put that in motion. I needed to talk to my brother first, make sure he didn't strike back at the Rosanos while I did my work. Get the go-ahead to tell at least the brothers what I'd discovered so the Hell Kickers would back off on the Nobles. I didn't have time to plan a subtle killing while a war was already swinging into full gear.

Besides, the brothers might want to deal with their former stepmom and her treachery their own way.

I watched Holly and Brant for a while longer, but all they did was talk, without any noticeable affection between them. Had she seduced him, or was this a purely professional arrangement? I guessed it didn't really matter either way.

When they got up to leave, I hustled away. I had to get in touch with Ezra before I made any further moves. Holly, the mastermind behind the disastrous deal—who would have thought?

This time, I strode right into the brownstone and up to my bedroom. Thankfully, I flicked on the light before moving toward my bag with its concealed phone, or I might not have noticed Lucan sitting in the chair near the window before he realized what I was up to.

I stalled in my tracks at the sight of him and folded my arms over my chest as he stood up. "What's with the repeat of the room invasion?"

He raised his eyebrows. "What's with the repeat of the night-time stealth mission? I didn't think you'd still feel the need to sneak around when we're on the same side now."

I rolled my eyes. "I didn't slip out the window this time, and I'm back way before midnight. I think you're tracking my movements a little too closely for someone who's supposedly on my side." Why was he still watching me that warily?

My stomach started to sink, but at the same time, Lucan's stern expression fell. He took a step closer to me and stopped with an embarrassed dip of his head.

"I'm sorry," he said. "Old habits—and I've always been the one who keeps the closest eye on things. If you were trying to figure out more about the war that's brewing, I'd have hoped you'd let us in on it."

I exhaled in a rush, his apology softening my momentary irritation. It was hard to be annoyed with Lucan in general when he thought so much like I did, always considering strategy and logistics. I'd have been wary of me too, even after everything we'd hashed out.

But I couldn't bring him in on what I'd learned yet, not until I was sure of how Ezra wanted to handle the situation. I could set even more havoc in motion if I moved too incautiously myself, and my first loyalty was to the Nobles.

I strolled a little closer to Lucan, letting a teasing smile play with my lips. Letting myself appreciate him in a way I'd tried to resist the last time he'd been in my bedroom: the sculpted lines of his handsome face, the definition of his lean form that showed through his fitted button-up and slacks. The passionate alertness in his dark brown eyes.

I'd told Darius I wasn't going to choose between the three of them. I was allowed to want all three of them now. And the last time Lucan had come into this room, I was the only one who'd gotten off. I could distract him from his questions and return the favor in a very enjoyable way.

"We can't make *every* action we take a group operation," I reminded him in a light tone. "I'm pretty sure you're not bringing me around for all of your business activities. If I find something I think you need to know, I'll fill you in."

His pupils dilated at my approach, and an answering heat trickled through my veins. "Nothing to report so far, then?" he asked, his voice dipping lower.

"Nothing," I agreed, hating the lie, and stopped when I was close enough to run my fingers down the front of his shirt. "But since you're already here... I'm sure we could find other ways to occupy ourselves."

He sucked in a breath. "Anthea..." But then he didn't seem to know what else to say.

I trailed my fingers back up his chest to the side of his neck, holding his gaze. My heart thumped in a heady rhythm, anticipation building inside me. "You seemed to have all kinds of things you wanted to do with me when you thought I was the enemy. Have you suddenly lost interest in screwing me now that you know I'm not trying to screw you over?"

His throat worked. "No. Not at all."

"Good." I stroked my fingertips down his neck and then skimmed them all the way to the waist of his pants. "Because I remember how much you liked one particular thing we can do together."

When I cupped my hand against his groin, I found him so hard that an eager twinge pulsed between my legs. I nudged him backward with my other hand. Lucan reached for me, grasping my hair, but I pushed him right down into the chair he'd recently vacated and sank down between his splayed knees.

His eyes widened. "Fuck. Anthea, you don't have to—"

"I want to," I interrupted. "I remember how much I liked doing this too."

I unzipped his fly and freed his rigid cock. Lucan tipped back his head with a groan as I circled the corded length with my fingers. His hips jerked with my experimental pump, but then he gripped my hair harder, stilling me.

"I want you to know—it isn't just screwing to me. It never was, even when I was angry with you. I—I haven't been with anyone in the last seven years. I never wanted anyone to have the chance to mess with my emotions the way you did… and I'm not sure I could have met anyone who'd have affected me as much as you do anyway."

I hesitated, the weight of his confession settling over me. Was he saying he was a *virgin*—one of the powerful Rosano brothers, at the age of twenty-four? Or maybe he'd had some teenage flings before our night together, when he and I hadn't gone farther than I'd been about to right now, and he'd simply been abstinent since then. Either way, it said a lot.

Guilt over my ulterior motives, however minor they might be, jabbed at me. "It isn't just screwing to me either," I said. "What I've had with the three of you—I can't imagine anything else comparing. But if you don't want to do this right now, if the issues between us are too fresh—"

"No," Lucan said hoarsely. "I'm not standing back while my brothers step in this time. I need you to know that I want you just as much as they do."

He tugged me forward, and I came. I wrapped my mouth around the head of his cock, reveling in both the mildly musky flavor of him and the rough sound that escaped his lips. At the swivel of my tongue, his hips jerked.

He'd been this responsive that first time too, when we'd all collided in the common room that night. Darius and Felix might have been the ones who'd sent me careening over the edge, but I'd loved the fact that I'd been able to do the same for Lucan, that his careful exterior had unraveled with the unpracticed movements of my mouth.

I wasn't so inexperienced now, and this was one blowjob I was more than happy to offer.

I sucked him farther down, squeezing the base of his cock and slicking my tongue around him. As I bobbed up and down, savoring every twitch and the taste of his precum, Lucan fisted my hair with both hands.

He started to rock in the chair, pumping into my mouth to match my pace with increasing wildness but never too much force. Lucan wasn't one for overt aggression. Which was why he hadn't demanded more from me that first time.

But he didn't hesitate to speak up for what he wanted now. His breath broke again when I grazed my teeth over the underside of his erection, and then he rasped, "This isn't enough. I need to be inside you. I need to feel you coming apart with me."

A giddy shiver tingled over my skin. Yes. That felt… more right than many things had in the past few years.

I would have asked if he had a condom on him, but he'd just admitted he hadn't fucked anyone in the past seven years, if ever. The one minor disobedience I'd gotten away with during my marriage was having a birth control implant surreptitiously inserted into my arm to make sure I wouldn't end up not just a bang maid to Clyde but an unwilling mother as well. I'd gotten thoroughly tested as soon as I'd left Clyde's house. Lucan and I didn't need any other protection.

I rose off the floor, yanking my panties off as I went, and climbed right onto the chair over Lucan. He dropped his hands from my hair to my hips, adjusting my position against me and groaning as his cock slid against my opening, already drenched for him.

He might not have gotten around in recent years, but he knew what he was after now. With one quick yank, he pulled me down onto him, thrusting upward to fill me completely.

I gasped, my head bowing next to his. "Fuck," he muttered into my hair. "Even more amazing than I imagined."

"You feel pretty fucking amazing too," I informed him, taking his shaft even deeper into me. I hadn't actually been penetrated like this in months, and his cock stretched me in all the right ways. Reminding me of why people *liked* doing this, of what I'd missed while I'd been stuck with a man who saw me as little more than a blow-up doll.

Lucan pulled my mouth to his. Our lips crashed together, muffling the eager sounds we both made. A minty flavor lingered on his tongue. He devoured my mouth as he pounded up into me and then twisted his head to the side.

"I don't know how long I can hold out," he admitted in a strained voice. "You feel so good."

"Touch me," I murmured into his ear. "I know you can get me there. You managed it with just your fingers the other night."

He chuckled raggedly at the memory and tucked his hand between us. The second he found my clit, I jerked forward over him with the additional burst of pleasure.

"Just like that," I muttered. "Just keep—fuck, yes. That's perfect."

He laughed again with pure delight, stroking me harder as we rocked together on the chair. It tilted back a couple of inches against the wall, but I wouldn't have cared if it'd collapsed under us. Every plunge of his cock and press of his fingers sent me spiraling closer and closer to my release—

"*Fuck*," he gritted out, his other hand clamping tight on my thigh, and the sound of his coming tipped me over the edge with him. I shuddered with the wave of bliss, feeling him empty himself inside me with a spurt of heat.

As my muscles sagged against him, Lucan wrapped me in an embrace more demanding than any gesture he'd made during the actual sex. He pressed a kiss to my temple and my cheek, holding me like he never wanted to let go of me.

I nestled my head in the crook of his shoulder, overwhelmed by the urge to give myself over that completely. To say I'd never leave.

Somehow these three men were starting to feel more like home than anything I had waiting for me back in Paradise Bend.

I just hoped they'd still feel the same way about me when I figured out how to explain what I'd found out here —and why I'd been digging into their business in the first place.

TWENTY

Anthea

IT WAS past eleven when Lucan left my room and I could finally get out my hidden phone, but I knew Ezra would still be up. My brother was somehow both night owl and early bird, alert whenever he needed to be—which, to be fair, he needed to be a lot when overseeing the Nobles' domain. I wasn't sure how much he managed to sleep these days.

I started music playing at a moderate volume on my regular phone to cover my voice in case there were any listening devices in the room and dialed Ezra's number. As I expected, he picked up after just a couple of rings.

"What is it?" he asked without preamble. "Is it done?"

I sank down on the floor with my back to the side of the bed. "I think I know who's responsible, but it's not what we thought. It doesn't seem as if the Hell Kickers are directly involved."

My brother let out a scoffing sound. "Not involved?

They stormed my operation in Brooklyn just a couple of days ago. Killed nearly every man in there."

"I know," I said, my chest tightening. "But that was them retaliating—harshly—because they think *you* betrayed them. And after everything I've seen here, I'm convinced that Marcel and his sons—and all the higher Hell Kickers men—believe you really did instigate the shootout during the deal meetup."

"That's ridiculous. *We* know we didn't, so obviously—"

"I think it was a third party." My heart hitched slightly at cutting my brother off, especially when he was clearly not in a good mood, but I had to fill him in properly. "The evidence shows that a shooter who wasn't with either group fired on the meetup from a nearby location. The goal was presumably to make both you and the Rosanos believe the other had turned against you while stealing the money and the goods for themselves."

Ezra paused. "You're sure of this?"

"I haven't completely confirmed it, but I'm as close to sure as I can get without having witnessed it. It's the only thing that remotely fits what I've found here. And I know who the third party was, as well."

"Then why haven't you dealt with them?" my brother demanded.

I inhaled slowly to steady my nerves. He was upset, but he *was* my brother. He'd trusted me to carry out this mission. I didn't have to be nervous of him the way I'd been with Dad.

"Because I believe the person who orchestrated the supposed double-cross is more closely connected to the Hell Kickers than to the Nobles," I said. "That the attack was mainly aimed at them, so I should loop the Rosanos in on the situation so they can decide how to best proceed. They know the players better than I could possibly work out while I'm here."

Ezra let out a rough guffaw. "I don't want you telling them anything. They could be elbow-deep in this shit. They know the players so well, it's personal, but they're completely innocent?"

"Yes. I have good reason to think that the person behind the plot is Marcel's ex-wife."

"*What?*" Ezra said, not hiding his shock.

"It all adds up," I said quickly. "She was always vying to become part of the business side of his life when they were married, and he continuously put her off. Then he shoved her aside for someone new. I found out that she spread lies about me the last time I was here—I don't know if you remember that I came home early that last summer? It was because of her. And I saw her talking with one of the lower-level Hell Kickers who's pretended to have nothing to do with the deal but just happens to be an excellent marksman with a grudge against his superiors."

"Anthea…" My brother let out a huff of breath. "You're obviously very invested in this theory. But let's be reasonable about this. You're telling me that a woman with no experience in our kind of work managed to screw over two major bosses? That's ridiculous."

"I know what I've seen," I broke in. "It's hardly impossible. Look at me."

"You're a rare case. And you haven't toppled any gang bosses, only taken down a decrepit old man—and it took you five years to do that. I understand you might like the idea of a woman getting the better of higher powers, but you can't let that color your judgment."

"I'm *not*." My heart was sinking fast. I'd known he might be skeptical, but I hadn't expected him to reject my report that quickly and completely. And his dismissal of my solution for Clyde stung more than I'd been prepared for.

Hell, it'd taken me five years partly because I'd had to wait for dear old Dad to kick the bucket before I could even start laying the groundwork. I'd taken particular time and care, staying under the domain of that asshole, so that *Ezra* didn't experience any disruption in his business affairs. Where was the gratitude for or even recognition of my sacrifice?

"Say nothing to the Rosanos about your silly theory," my brother went on, his voice cold. "Get your head on straight the way I know it can be and figure out who's *really* behind this mess. And soon, because I'm gearing up for a counterattack here, and I'd rather you weren't caught in the crossfire."

He didn't say I wouldn't be, though. He didn't say he'd make sure to get me out before his retaliation put me in danger. My throat tightened, my jaw clenching.

How could I make him understand that I knew what I was talking about?

"Ezra, you have to—" I started, forgetting caution in that moment and speaking just a little louder than before —and of course at that exact moment, the door whipped open behind me.

I jerked around, hanging up the call and flicking the

phone under the bed. It was too late. Darius stormed inside, his eyes narrowing, his brothers right behind him.

"Ezra?" he repeated. "You were just talking to your brother? Your backstabbing brother who supposedly kicked you out of the house because he had no use for you?"

His voice was cool but not brutal—yet. I scrambled for an explanation. "I—"

"Let's look for it first," Lucan said before I could find the right words, striding past Darius and scanning the room. *His* tone was outright icy, a sharp contrast to the way he'd spoken to me right before I'd wrapped my lips around his cock just an hour ago.

I assumed he meant the phone. There wasn't much I could do to hide it. He stalked over to the bed and peered underneath it, but he didn't grab the device like I'd expected. Felix went to the end table and opened the drawer there, and Darius checked the closet.

I stood up, frowning. "What are you looking for?"

"Oh, we got a report from some dork," Felix said, only a slight edge in his breezy voice. It sounded like he, at least, wasn't very concerned. "Saying you pilfered something from the family stash. Why you'd ever want to—"

Lucan had just lifted the mattress up from the frame. "It's here," he said, cutting Felix off.

The younger guy froze. "What?"

Lucan lifted up a figurine that'd been tucked under the mattress—a narrow, golden statuette of a woman with streaming hair and her hands pressed to her chest. He shot me an accusing look, his mouth twisting.

I blinked at the figurine. "I don't know why you're looking at me like that. I have no idea what that is or what it's doing in here. It's probably been there since before I took this room."

Darius stepped closer, studying the figurine and then me. "Then why did one of our guys say he saw you carrying it into your room?"

"I don't know!" I said. "But whoever it was, they were lying. What's so special about that thing anyway?"

"Maybe you just saw something you could hawk for cash," Lucan said in the same icy tone as before. "But this belonged to our mother."

Oh, shit. I'd known Marcel kept a bunch of things belonging to his first wife—the guys' mom—around the house. When we'd been teens, Felix had shown me a bookcase full of her old books and trinkets in Marcel's lounge room. There wasn't anything all that sentimental about it for their dad, who'd more than moved on as far as I'd been able to tell, but he felt the need to give his sons a sense of their entire family legacy.

The brothers hadn't known their mother very well. Unlike all Marcel's other wives since, she'd died rather than being ditched—a sudden, aggressive cancer when Darius had only been five. Felix had admitted to me once that he didn't even remember her. He'd only been two when she passed on, after all. Her loss was a scar they all bore, and they'd have defended her memory fiercely if they needed to. Including her actual belongings.

I held up my hands in a gesture of surrender. "I swear I didn't touch that. I had no idea it was in here. I'm not desperate for money—I already hawked a few pieces that were my late husband's."

"Then what's it doing here?" Darius demanded.

"I have no idea. It's not like the Hell Kickers are feeling all that friendly toward the Nobles right now. Maybe someone wants me gone."

"The guy who tipped us off wasn't part of any operations to do with the Nobles," Lucan said. "And you *were* just talking to your brother, weren't you?"

Triple shit. In my confusion, I'd almost forgotten the conversation they'd walked in on.

"And what's so horrible about that?" I shot back. "I'm not allowed to try and figure out a way you all could make peace with him so that this war doesn't go any further?" That wasn't even a lie. That was essentially what I'd been trying to convince Ezra to do, in a roundabout way.

"He took your call," Darius said ominously. "You had some secret phone ready to dial him up on?" He grabbed my regular phone off my bed and turned off the music. "And you were trying to cover up the fact that you were talking to him." Rage and hurt shone together in his eyes. "Why did you really come here, Anthea?"

My heart wrenched. Everything I'd been juggling since I'd arrived was tumbling down, and suddenly I couldn't bear to dig the hole any deeper.

These men deserved at least part of the truth. I wasn't going to betray Ezra, but that didn't mean I couldn't betray myself.

"I've been trying to figure out what really did happen the night that deal went wrong," I admitted, speaking quickly. "Investigating the people involved. I can't believe my brother would turn on your family like that. And I've found proof that—"

Felix's face had tightened. "You weren't spying on us seven years ago, but you are now," he cut in. "Fucking hell."

"It's my family. You'd do the same. I know the three of *you* didn't do anything wrong, or I wouldn't have— I'm just making sure you have the full story—"

"I think we do now," Darius growled. His fury was practically vibrating off him. He clenched his hands at his sides and then jabbed one finger toward the door. "Get out."

I stared at him. "What?"

"Get. Out. Grab you shit and get the hell out of our sight. Your fucking 'investigation' ends here. Go running back to your brother if he'll have you or figure out something for yourself, but we're not keeping a rat in our home."

My pulse stuttered. After everything he'd admitted to me—

But that was why he was so furious, wasn't it? Because he'd cared, he'd let himself fall for me again, and I really had deceived him this time. People who were wounded when they were feeling vulnerable went even farther onto the defensive than they might have otherwise.

This couldn't have happened in a worse way if Holly had planned it herself.

My spine stiffened. Part of me wanted to stay and fight, but I had the feeling I wasn't going to win. Not with my words alone, anyway. I needed proof—to convince both Ezra and the three men standing around me that I knew what I was talking about and that it was a good thing I'd dug deeper.

"Fine." I grabbed my duffel bag, which I'd kept packed in case I needed to make a hasty exit, and slung my purse over my shoulder. "But you need to know that things aren't how they look. I'm going to confirm what I'm already almost sure of, and then you'll be hearing from me again."

"Don't you dare—"

"I'm going!" I shot back, and marched past Darius out of the room.

I didn't stop walking until I'd gone down the stairs and out the front door. It was fully dark outside, pitch-black between the streams of lamplight. I closed my eyes, gathered my resolve, and strode onward.

I'd figure this out. I'd show them; I'd make them understand.

I'd better, because my heart already felt like it'd been broken in two all over again. And this time it might be my fault, not theirs.

———

I managed to find myself a grungy hotel room, slept for a few hours, and then started digging around online. When my efforts didn't produce anything to my satisfaction, I called up Wylder, since it wasn't as if my connections to my family could be any more exposed now that I wasn't even in the Rosano home.

"Auntie Anthea," he said in his teasing tone, way

cockier than any seventeen-year-old had a right to be. "What's going on?"

"I was actually hoping that computer genius friend of yours could do a little hacking on my behalf," I said.

Wylder laughed. "Oh, I'm not good enough for you now? I'll find Gideon. He'll probably break out the champagne to celebrate getting picked over me."

"When you learn how to work computers like he does, I'll come to you for my digital needs," I said dryly.

Three hours later, I'd hired myself a rental car and gotten the address of Holly Eisener's most recent apartment in the city. After that, it was a waiting game.

I tailed Holly when I spotted her platinum pixie cut behind the wheel of the Camry that Gideon had also determined was registered to her name. She had a very banal day of driving to the dry cleaner's and the gym and then an office where she had a short shift as a receptionist. Then she drove back to her apartment building.

I was just considering giving up for the night when the Camry eased out of the parking garage long after the streetlamps had flickered on. I drove behind her as she wove through the streets and out to a stretch of warehouses along the river. She cruised around the back of a small concrete building.

I parked my rental farther down the street and paused to pull on my thin jacket that I'd already prepped for particularly dangerous operations. A tiny pistol was tucked into a nook at the wide base of one of the flowy sleeves, a few needles discreetly hidden in the other.

Stepping out of the car, I smoothed the skirt of my dress flat as if that would soothe my jittering nerves too.

Then I slunk over to the building through the darkness. When I reached the lot behind the warehouse, the view in front of me told all the story I needed.

Holly had gotten out of the car and walked over to a garage-style door at the back of the building, which was now open. A light had come on overtop of it. She was standing there, peering at stacks of boxes, several of them with manufacturer names printed on them. I recognized them as companies Ezra often used as a front. She had her hands on her hips and her head tilted to the side as if she were sizing them up, though for what, I wasn't sure.

She hadn't managed to move all of the merchandise yet. I guessed that wasn't surprising. Brant didn't have the kind of reach to unload a huge shipment of that much value all at once—definitely not without the other Hell Kickers catching wind of it.

I snapped a few silent photos with my phone. Would even that be enough proof for Ezra?

I wavered for several seconds, and then I skimmed through my contacts to find Felix's number. He was the only one who'd bothered to make sure I had it after our reconciliation the other day—for the same reasons that he was the one I'd have wanted to reach out to anyway. He wasn't inclined to hold grudges unless it was absolutely necessary.

My brother had asked me not to tell the Rosanos about my suspicions, but I didn't see any betrayal in ensuring they found the evidence for themselves and drew their own conclusions.

The three of you should get down here ASAP, I texted him, and included my current location. *You'll find out everything you need to know about who you should really be pissed off at.*

What are you talking about? he wrote back moments later. *What crazy shit are you trying to drag us into now?*

I'm trying to make sure you see the truth. Unless you're not interested in that after all. Anyway, since when did you mind crazy?

There was a longer pause. The dots appeared, showing Felix was typing. I peered down at the phone, willing the words to hurry up and appear—and the hard muzzle of a gun pressed against the back of my head.

"Throw that phone away, *now*," Brant's voice said from right behind me.

TWENTY-ONE

Felix

I SHOULDN'T HAVE CARED about any woman like this. Maybe if I told myself I didn't enough times, it would sink in. That's how brains worked, right?

Not so much, it seemed.

We'd all come up to our apartment together after grabbing dinner, unstated tension still simmering between us. I was sitting on the sofa in the common room, flipping the quarter I always carried in my pocket over and over. Normally I used it to decide which of two options that seemed equally exciting I should pursue. Right now I felt like I had no options at all, but something about the flicking motion kept me vaguely distracted.

Darius had gone into his bedroom. The booming of a hip hop beat that reverberated through the door said all I needed to know about his mood. He drowned himself in rhythms and aggressive lyrics when he was particularly peeved and trying to detach himself from the world around him.

Lucan had sat down at the desk across from me, because of course he had. He was flipping through a notebook and scrawling a few words in it here and there, but every couple of minutes he stopped and looked at the gold figurine he'd set off to the side of the wooden surface. I didn't think he was seeing anything useful in its gleaming form, but each time his mouth tightened a little more.

"It doesn't make any sense," I said abruptly, because I'd never known how to keep my mouth shut.

Lucan lifted his gaze to consider me a lot the same way he had the statuette. "What?" he asked, as if he couldn't figure out what I was talking about.

I rolled my eyes at him, pretending more nonchalance than I actually felt. "Her stealing that thing. It didn't seem like she was hurting that badly for cash. There was plenty in her wallet when I checked her purse the other night when we went looking for her. And even if she was, you said she'd just gone out yesterday evening—why wouldn't she have sold it then instead of leaving it in her room where she could get caught?"

I hadn't thought I was talking that loudly, but apparently Darius's hearing was better than I'd anticipated. The hip hop abruptly cut out, and his door swung open. "What are you going on about?" he demanded in a terse voice.

I hadn't meant to bring him into the conversation— well, technically I hadn't really thought through having the conversation at all—but I guessed I was stuck now.

"We know Anthea's a smart cookie," I said. "Nothing about the theft makes any sense."

Lucan sighed. "You're making too many assumptions. She might have tried to sell it last night and not found a buyer, so she brought it back and hid it again. She might have known she had a buyer but not been able to arrange the hand-off quickly enough."

"She might have been planning to take it on a trip to Mars," I shot back. "How the hell does it make any sense for her to steal *that* anyway? Anyone in the family could recognize it at a glance. If she'd grabbed something more generic, like a watch or one of the diamond rings, she could have made a case that it was hers. Heck, a ring would've been a lot easier to hide, too."

"Maybe she didn't see a watch or the rings," Darius growled. "It doesn't matter. We've been over this. The most important thing is that she came here under false pretenses, looking to dig up information for her brother to use against us. If she was willing to lie to our faces like that, put on such a good act, who knows what else she's capable of?"

We had talked about that before. He had made very similar points. But they still didn't sit totally right with me.

Darius glowered at me. "You've got to stop thinking so much with your dick, Felix. Holly was right about her, even if she was seven years early with her accusations. We should have steered clear no matter what sob story Anthea gave us."

It was true that one of the images that kept darting through my mind was the feel of Anthea's hand around my cock while I'd had her pinned against the wall just across the room. The little breathy noises she'd let spill out of her with more abandon now that she hadn't been pretending to be unaffected like she had during our coat-closet interlude. The smell of her, the *taste* of her… so much more of her I'd wanted to taste but hadn't gotten the chance to yet…

But that didn't matter either. It didn't matter that she drew me to her like I was a moth and she was the flame, tangling up my emotions in ways no other woman ever had. Except—

"Do you really think it was just a sob story?" I said. "You were pretty convinced after you talked to her that she was telling the truth about her husband. And her take on what happened with Holly made a hell of a lot more sense than what we'd figured. She *sounded* like she really was confused and angry at us."

"She was probably telling the truth about both of those things," Lucan put in with flat certainty. "That doesn't mean she wasn't using the truth to steer us away from other truths she didn't want us seeing."

I frowned. "She said she was trying to settle the war and make peace. I don't like that she lied to us, but do you really think she was trying to hurt us?"

"She was trying to stop her fuckwad brother from getting hurt," Darius muttered.

Maybe that was also true. But I was pretty sure the two men in the room with me sometimes—maybe even often—saw *me* as their fuckwad brother, and yet they'd still be there for me no matter what.

Anthea had also said we'd have done the same to her if

our positions were reversed. I wasn't sure she was wrong about that. After all, we'd launched a campaign against her over something that'd happened seven years ago when she was only sixteen, banding together without hesitation to run her through the wringer.

The decision had blown up in our faces, but I couldn't see how that was *her* fault.

I sucked my lip under my teeth, resisting the urge to gnaw at it. I didn't know how to get those thoughts across to my brothers in a way they'd listen to. I wasn't any kind of authority figure between the three of us.

But I did know that for the whole day with Anthea gone, not knowing what was happening to her or where she was now, a hole inside me that I hadn't even known was there had only yawned wider and emptier.

Why the fuck were we being so protective of the whole family anyway? *Dad* had screwed us over by listening to that Griffin prick rather than his own sons, by cutting us out of his plans. And all Darius cared about was getting back into his good graces instead of recognizing that the old man's respect maybe wasn't worth what it used to be?

The thought of Griffin gave me pause. I glanced at Lucan. "You said it was a pretty minor underling who came to you about seeing Anthea with the figurine. Who was it exactly?" He hadn't mentioned names earlier, and I hadn't asked because it hadn't seemed important. It wasn't like I'd expected to put the name to a face anyway. But Lucan would remember. Keeping track of the details was his thing.

As expected, he answered without missing a beat. "A guy named Brant. He's been with the Hell Kickers for about four years now. Pretty average foot soldier, has a couple of side connections that've been useful once or twice."

Brant. A jolt of horror hit me. There'd been that guy—coming out of Dad's lounge—I'd known his name was something with a B.

"Is he kind of on the short side, with curly hair?" I asked tentatively.

Lucan gave me an odd look. "That's the one. I'm surprised you paid enough attention."

Fuck. Now the emptiness inside me had been filled in with a wave of nausea.

"And where was that figurine before?" I asked, dreading the answer, with a nod toward the desk. "Where was Dad keeping it that Anthea would have supposedly stolen it from?"

Darius broke in before Lucan could answer. "It was in the bookcase in the lounge room near his office where he's got a bunch of Mom's old stuff. Why do you care?"

I swallowed hard. "Because just a few days ago, I saw that Brant guy coming out of the lounge room looking shifty, like he knew he'd done something wrong. He said Dad had wanted him to grab a book for him, but that seemed strange to me."

Lucan's brow knit. "And you didn't press him about it?"

I threw up my hands. "I didn't think there was any reason to make a commotion about it! I did ask a couple of questions, and he acted like it was no big deal, so I thought I'd read him wrong. And I had no idea I had to be worried about him framing our guests for theft."

Because that's what had happened here, clearly. Brant had nabbed the figurine and stashed it under Anthea's mattress sometime when she'd been out of the room. And then he'd tattled on her.

I pushed myself off the sofa with a surge of frustrated adrenaline. "Why would he have wanted to set her up? What would *he* have against her?"

Finally, my brothers didn't have an immediate retort. Darius and Lucan glanced at each other and then at me. Darius's grim expression had taken on a more puzzled cast.

"He could have some beef with the Nobles that we don't know about," he said slowly.

"Or he thought he would win points with Dad by supposedly catching her in a betrayal," Lucan added. "There are plenty of reasons. None of it discounts—"

My phone pinged with an incoming text. My forehead furrowed. I didn't give out my main number to many people, and two of the few who had it were already in the room with me.

I dug it out of my pocket, and my pulse hiccupped. "It's Anthea."

I half expected Darius to make a cutting remark about the fact that I'd shared my number with *her*, but both of my brothers stayed silent as I read her text. She'd sent a location from near the river, with the words, *The three of you should get down here ASAP. You'll find out everything you need to know about who you should really be pissed off at.*

What kind of message was that? I'd been sitting here trying to defend her, and she sent me some vague-ass call-to-arms?

My thumbs were already tapping on the screen as I

gave my report. "She says we can find out who's causing the real problem if we meet her someplace by the river. No details."

What are you talking about? I wrote. *What crazy scheme are you trying to drag us into now?* Darius and Lucan would never let me hear the end of it if I convinced them to believe in her and then things only turned out worse.

"She'd better give some details," Darius growled, stepping closer as if he could intimidate her through the screen.

Her reply didn't get us very far. *I'm trying to make sure you see the truth. Unless you're not interested in that after all. Anyway, since when did you mind crazy?*

I scowled at the screen, wondering how to reply to that. Why couldn't she just say what the hell was going on? *Crazy is fine as long as I know what's in the mix. What are you doing over there? What is it you want us to see, exactly?*

There, even Lucan couldn't complain about my meticulousness now. I sent the text and sat back down on the arm of the sofa as I waited.

There was nothing, not even the dots to indicate she was typing. Then all of a sudden, a nonsensical jumble of characters leapt onto the screen from her end. *Gkhjilu*

Either your autocorrect has been possessed by a demon or you're dodging the question, I replied.

Nothing. One minute stretched into another, and there was no sign she was on the other end.

A chill crept down my back. I turned my phone to show it to my brothers. Lucan got up from his desk to take a closer look.

"She was out doing more of her investigating, looking into whoever she thinks is really to blame for the double-cross, and now she's gone quiet," I said, hoping I didn't have to spell out why this seemed like bad news.

Lucan swiped his hand across his mouth. "That combination of characters looks like she could have been jabbing her thumb over the screen keypad as quickly as possible, just to send something."

"Like she realized she was in deep shit and didn't have time to say so," I filled in.

"Yes."

"Fuck." Darius heaved a breath, his arms folding over his chest so the muscles bulged. Then the cool, commanding vibe that I'd always admired in him even when it pissed me off filled out his stance. "We have to go. We have to find out what's happened to her—and what she's uncovered."

"And make sure she's still alive to tell us about it," Lucan said, paling.

As angry as we all had been, it was good to know none of us actually wanted her dead. I leapt back to my feet. "Then let's get moving!"

Whatever we found, I had the feeling it was going to answer all our questions. Hopefully we wouldn't regret the way we'd forced this crisis to a head.

TWENTY-TWO

Anthea

BRANT PROBABLY ASSUMED I'd be too freaked out by having a gun pointed at me to do anything other than stand there like a deer in the headlights. He had no idea how many weapons I'd already stared down in my twenty-three years.

My phone dinged with an incoming text. I'd already lowered my hand; I couldn't risk even the movement of lifting it to check what Felix had said. It probably wouldn't make any difference to my current dilemma anyway.

I jerked my thumb across the touchpad as quickly as I could. I couldn't compose a coherent message, but if I could send *something* that would indicate to Felix that the situation had turned sour—

Brant walloped my wrist with his free hand, sending the phone clattering across the pavement. I couldn't tell whether I'd managed to hit enter in time. He shoved me after it with the gun still at the back of my skull and stomped on the screen for good measure. The crunch of the internal circuitry fracturing made me wince internally.

Well, I definitely wasn't chatting up anyone on that thing again.

While he was focused on destroying the phone, I flicked one of the needles tucked into my left sleeve into my grasp and jerked my hand past him as if trying to free myself. I scraped him with the toxin-laced tip lightly enough that he'd think it was just my fingernails.

Brant swung around, outright smacking me with the gun across the side of my head. Pain splintered through my skull, and I couldn't suppress a gasp. Stumbling without needing to fake it, I let the needle fall with the rasp of my feet on the asphalt to cover the sound.

I couldn't lace a tip that tiny with enough of anything subtle that would completely spin this encounter in my favor, but getting that jab in might have bought me a big enough opening to turn the tide. My hand itched to reach for the gun in my right sleeve, but with the muzzle of Brant's pistol still pressed against my scalp, I knew I wouldn't get far with it. Not yet.

I had to save my few secret advantages for when I could make the best possible use of them.

Holly had spun around at the noise of our scuffle. "What the fuck is going on?" she snapped at Brant under her breath in a tone that confirmed my suspicions that there was no personal affection between the two of them.

"It's the Noble bitch," Brant said. He prodded me toward Holly and the stacked boxes beyond the doorway, not caring about how I winced when the pistol's muzzle bumped the tender spot where he'd bashed me earlier.

"She tracked you here somehow. I told you that we had to be careful."

"Maybe she tracked *you*," Holly snarked back. They made such a cohesive team. She narrowed her eyes at me. "What are you doing here, you stupid girl?"

I gave her a tight smile, keeping my fingers curled inside the jacket's wide sleeves. "I should be asking you that, I think, considering that the stuff behind you belongs to either my brother or the Hell Kickers depending on how you look at it. It definitely doesn't belong to you."

"Finders, keepers, isn't that how it goes?" she said in an arch tone.

"I don't think you exactly *found* that shipment," I replied dryly.

Holly scowled at me, probably annoyed that I wasn't cowering at their feet. She'd have to break my knees before I ended up down on the pavement.

"Where's your other accomplice?" I went on, figuring I might as well drag whatever information I could out of them by playing clueless while I had the chance. It'd also be helpful to know if I should be prepared for any other men with guns to turn up out of the blue.

Brant rapped me with the gun. "What are you talking about?"

"That Griffin dude. Isn't he in on this with you? He sure seems keen on the whole war thing."

The guy behind me snorted. "That fucking idiot doesn't have any more clue than the rest of them. Just another bootlicker. Worked in our favor, though, pushing Marcel along like that."

I forced my eyes wide. "You and Holly pulled this off all by yourselves?"

"Don't sound so surprised," Holly sneered. "No one in that fucking house ever gave me the chance I deserved."

So it really was just these two coming up with the scheme on their own. Well, I suspected Holly had done most of the thinking. Brant was the muscle—and the gun.

"Were you really so peeved about Marcel divorcing you that you had to pull this?" I asked her, partly out of honest curiosity. "I mean, you were wifey number three. You didn't figure that was a bad sign from the get-go?"

Holly bared her teeth at me, her pretty face transforming into something hard and a little unhinged. "I could have stood right beside him properly if he'd let me prove myself. He was only looking for arm candy, it turns out. So I'll just have to build my own empire."

Holy hell, the delusions ran even deeper with this woman than I'd imagined. She wasn't just out to undermine two major gangs—she figured she was going to start her own with her ill-gotten gains? With this shithead Brant as her right-hand man?

But even as I scoffed internally, I had to admit she hadn't gotten off to a totally bad start. She'd set two major powers in this part of the country at each other's throats, ready to tear away at one another—and maybe she figured she could fill in the gaps they left.

There was something kind of thrilling about the idea of a woman in charge of a syndicate like the Nobles or the Hell Kickers. If it'd been a different woman, if it hadn't meant the potential destruction of my own family's legacy, I might have cheered her on.

But this was a vindictive cunt who'd savaged the heart of a sixteen-year-old girl for no reason that couldn't have been entirely selfish. Someone that petty wasn't going to be any kind of role model.

"Wonderful," I said. "I wouldn't have intervened if you hadn't involved my family in the whole mess."

Holly sniffed disdainfully. "As if you didn't involve yourself in *my* life way before now. Who do you figure you're fooling with that cutesy dress? You think I don't know why your dad kept sending you under Marcel's eye? Practically offering you up on a platter. He figured he'd get the hook in good and deep, and as soon as you were old enough—"

She snapped her fingers. Then a malicious smirk crossed her face. "I wonder what Marcel would think if he knew what a whore you were even back then."

A shudder crawled down my spine. *That* was why she'd poisoned the years of friendship and budding love between me and the Rosano brothers—because she assumed Dad had been setting me up for Marcel? The guy might have liked his women young, but I'd never gotten the impression he saw me that way. Ugh. I'd only been ten years old when I had my first summer visit.

But this woman clearly didn't have any concept of normal human thought patterns.

Brant tapped me on the head with the side of his pistol again. "It's none of your business anyway. Your idiot brother didn't want you. You're a goddamn stray. No one's going to miss you when you're gone."

The blatant threat made my skin prickle even more. I

braced myself, studying the scene and working out my options. If I could just delay them a little longer…

But I didn't want to wait for the Rosano brothers to show up, if they were even on their way after my conversation with Felix. I wasn't some damsel in distress needing rescue. I was Anthea fucking Noble, and I took care of my own business.

I'd needed to deal with these two, and it appeared I was going to have to do it much faster than I'd have preferred if I was going to get out of this alive. But it'd had to happen either way.

It would be better—simpler—if no one suspected anyone other than these two had ever been here. No investigation into their connections, which would bring a heap of police trouble down on the Rosanos' heads. No possible fingers pointed at me, just months after a different death.

Could I pull off an even bigger con than I ever had before, without weeks to plan every variable? Maybe, if the pieces I'd set in motion came together properly. From the corner of my eye, I thought I caught a slight sway in Brant's stance. The toxin had gotten several minutes to travel through his bloodstream. His muscles shouldn't be holding him up quite as firmly as they normally would.

"You don't have to kill me," I said, holding up my hands. "And if you do, believe me, my brother won't be happy about that. How many enemies are you looking to collect?"

"Cast-off gang princess," Holly sneered at me. "Who says anyone will ever know what happened to you? We'll make you completely disappear."

That could be the prompt I needed. "Vanishing a person isn't all that easy," I said, taking on a haughty tone I knew would irk her. "Especially someone like me."

Holly stalked closer to me and looked me up and down. She waved Brant to the side, and he stepped back with his gun still aimed at my head.

Perfect. I'd bought myself a little more space to work with.

"Let me guess, you've got something on you that you expect the Nobles to trace," she said with obvious skepticism. She patted my sides and my pockets, shoving her hands right into the latter to check for phones or other devices.

"She was doing something on the phone I broke when I caught her," Brant said, jerking his head toward the spot where he'd smashed it.

Holly glared at me. "What were you up to? Were you talking to someone?"

I stared steadily back at her. "Why should I tell you?"

She hissed through her teeth and turned toward Brant —exactly where I needed her. "You shouldn't have crushed it. Go and—"

My pulse thumped faster with a jolt of adrenaline. Before she could finish her order, I snatched the little pistol out of my sleeve, whipped my arm in front of her chest, and shot three bullets into Brant's torso.

Holly let out a shriek. She grabbed at me, but I was already darting away and past her. Brant staggered, blood blooming across his chest, but his gun arm managed to follow me.

Thankfully, my toxin was slowing him down, messing

with his reflexes. His arm wobbled, and then I was on him.

I caught his hand in mine, yanked it up, and squeezed his finger on the trigger.

The bullet caught Holly in the neck. I'd been aiming for her head, but the slight deviation would do given the circumstances. She gurgled, blood gushing from the artery I'd hit.

Brant swore, but the words mingled with a groan of pain. He slumped to his knees. Holly teetered, clamping her hand to her neck ineffectually. Blood spurted from beneath her fingers. She shot daggers at me with her eyes, but the life was already fading from them.

I stepped well back, wiping my pistol on the fabric of my jacket to remove my fingerprints. "If you're thinking that I'm going to pay for this, you can forget about that. No one's going to have any idea this was anything other than a spat between lovers with criminal inclinations. I'll be removing every sign that I was here before I leave, and the cops aren't going to look too closely when the obvious evidence will add right up."

She opened her mouth, but all that sputtered out was more blood. Swaying, she keeled right over. The life had left her before she even hit the ground. Her corpse sprawled there, limbs akimbo, her hair more scarlet than ice-blond now.

Brant had slumped onto his chest. I fought the urge to put one more bullet in his brain, just to be sure. That would only make the police *un*sure of how this spat had gone down. His breath rasped and then stopped.

As I checked his pulse, confirming it'd stopped, an

engine roared nearby. Tires screeched, and a dark sports car careened around the warehouse into the lot.

Before I could do more than tense up, braced for a bigger fight, all three of the Rosano brothers spilled out into the night.

TWENTY-THREE

Anthea

THE THREE BROTHERS stopped in their tracks in front of the open car doors, staring at me and the scene around me.

"What the *fuck*?" Darius said. "We heard shots…"

I raised my chin, looking right back at them, and motioned to Holly, who'd sagged totally limp into the pool of her blood, her eyes staring blankly. "There's the mastermind behind the shootout at the deal hand-off, such as she currently is. And there's the guy who took the first shots, making both sides think the other was attacking them." I pointed to Brant.

Felix was outright gaping. "And you just…"

I helpfully filled in the blanks. "This is what everyone is going to know happened: Holly and Brant got into an argument about what to do with all the crap they stole from you and my brother." Careful to stay clear of the blood on the ground, I walked over to Holly, crouched down, and tucked my gun into her hand. "The gunshot residue will fit, as will the angles of the shots. Enough that no one's going to bother to look more closely, anyway. I made it the cleanest job I could within the many limitations."

"And what really happened?" Lucan asked quietly.

As I straightened up, I gave him a coy look. "Didn't I just tell you?" I rubbed the side of my head where Brant had whacked me with his gun and winced. It didn't feel sore enough to warrant concussion worries, but I was definitely going to have a bruise there. "Maybe given the fact that they're here and so's your stuff, this once you'll take my word on the rest."

Lucan's eyebrows arched slightly. "You set it up so there wouldn't be any heat on us."

I shrugged. "Whatever you think of me, I've never wanted to screw you over. If I can do a job clean, then that's how I work."

Felix let out a disbelieving guffaw. Darius gave a huff of breath and strode toward me. I stiffened all over again, but all he did was wrap his arms around me and squeeze me close.

"I thought you were getting fucking *killed*," he growled.

The demanding pressure of the embrace steadied me. "*I* thought you'd be happier about that possibility, considering how we left things."

"No," he said hoarsely. "No fucking way. I just— finding out, after everything—" He pulled back to look at the bodies and then back at me, his eyes blazing with emotion. "You're a goddamn marvel, Lady Noble. And this is the last time you're going anywhere without me."

"Er, shouldn't I get some say—"

He cut me off with the crash of his mouth against mine, and for that moment, I decided I'd go along with his terms. We could hash out the details later.

I kissed him back with everything I had, my body waking up in an instant as if it'd been waiting just for this my whole life. Darius tugged my body flush with his, the bulge of his groin unignorable.

I was vaguely aware of his brothers drawing closer around us. Felix cleared his throat. Darius kissed me again, almost tenderly, and then raised his head to glower at the younger guy.

"Maybe there should be some apologies before the passionate mauling continues," Felix said wryly. As his gaze darted to me, his mouth twisted. "Starting with me. We seem to keep getting tangled up in misunderstandings and miscommunication. I should have spoken up for you sooner—before these two bullied you out of the house."

My throat tightened. "I get it," I said, letting my gaze hold his before looking at Lucan and Darius again. "I was hiding things, and that was a sore spot for you, especially after the lies we'd only just cleared up. But I swear I only wanted to take down the people who actually hurt you and the Nobles. I'd like to see the alliance between my family and yours back in place if that's possible. I'm not here to wage war."

"Only on the people who deserved it," Lucan said, glancing down at Holly and Brant. "I can't help thinking we're lucky you haven't decided we deserve retribution too."

The corner of my lips quirked upward. "I'm sure you could get there if you tried really hard."

He smiled back, cautious but I thought more out of fear of saying the wrong thing than because he was wary of me anymore. "I think I like being on your side a whole lot better. Or on top of you. Or under you. I'm pretty open to the possibilities, if you still are."

I motioned him closer, and he rested a hand on my waist. Then I met Darius's eyes.

The eldest Rosano brother's face had darkened. He tipped his head to rest his forehead against mine. "I'm going to lead the Hell Kickers one day. I should be a better man than I've been to you. I promise I don't normally let my temper get the better of me like that. If you want to yell at me a while to even the score, have at it."

I touched his cheek. "Yelling is definitely not what I want to do with you. I just need to know that we're good now. No more worries about my loyalties?"

He paused. "Is it going to be a problem, being with us and being true to your family at the same time? We don't know that Ezra won't want his own retribution no matter what you tell him."

I didn't even need to think to know my answer. "I'll only stand with my family when they deserve it too. My brother doesn't have me on a leash—I make my own rules." At least, I did from now on. After what I'd just survived, there wasn't a single part of me that was willing to jump at *anyone's* command anymore, even my brother's.

Darius exhaled roughly. "I wasn't worried about that. I

don't think you'd turn on us for his gain—hell, you already had the perfect opportunity if you'd been interested in going there. I just don't want to ruin *your* life so I can have you in mine."

An ache formed around my heart, but it wasn't an unpleasant one. "The three of you haven't been ruining my life," I said softly. "You're reminding me how to live for myself again. And I'm not letting anyone take what's mine away from me ever again."

"We're yours," Lucan said without hesitation. "As long as you'll have us."

"So let's get on with making you ours," Darius growled. "We've waited too long as it is. We'll fucking christen the site of your victory."

He hefted my petite frame against his brawny one in a single smooth movement and marched me past the fallen bodies into the deeper shadows of the storage area. As he set me on a box where my legs could splay around his waist, I curled my fingers into his shirt and tipped my head back to welcome his kiss.

It really was the perfect place to reclaim everything that'd been ours for one brief night years ago, that the woman lying dead a few feet away had nearly stolen from us forever, along with everything else she'd robbed us of.

We were never going to be easy people, any of us. We'd been broken and brutal with each other, and we all had our sharp edges still. But the slate was clear now, no more secrets or resentments left between us. Just me and the men some part of me had always known were meant to be by my side. The fierceness of our hearts fit together just right.

All three of those men surrounded me now. Lucan came around Darius to tuck his hand around my waist, peeling back my jacket so he could kiss the bare skin of my upper arm beneath. Felix clambered right up on the boxes next to me and pressed his lips to the top of my head as he eased the jacket off my other arm.

"It's getting cool out," he murmured, "but we're going to keep you nice and hot."

A giddy giggle that wasn't at all like me tumbled from my throat against Darius's lips. He kissed me harder and then pulled back just an inch. "I love hearing you like that. But there are all kinds of other sounds I want to hear from that mouth too."

I peered at him through my eyelashes. "You'll get what you deserve."

He grinned. "Then I'd better get on with earning those moans."

He tugged the jacket right off me, and Felix wasted no time jerking down the zipper at the back of my dress. The guys didn't hesitate to make good on his promise to warm me up. They all leaned closer, Darius capturing my mouth again while his hands roamed down my sides, Felix nibbling my neck and teasing his fingers over the curve of one breast, Lucan cupping the other with a flick of his thumb over my pebbling nipple.

Quivers of pleasure raced through my nerves from every direction. I couldn't restrain a whimper, arching into their combined touch.

It was so much better than the first time. Better because I wasn't that hesitant teen girl who'd been afraid she'd embarrass herself. Better because we all knew this wasn't just one night. We were in this thing together, for as long as the world didn't manage to tear us apart.

Darius lowered his head abruptly, searing a path over my jaw and down my neck. Felix took the opportunity to turn my face toward him and plant his lips on mine. As his tongue darted blissfully into my mouth, Lucan worked his own kind of magic fondling my breast and squeezing my ass.

I gave a little growl of encouragement, my panties dampening. Darius dropped low enough to yank down my bra and bring his mouth to the breast Felix had released. His tongue swiveled around the peak in perfect symphony with the movements of Felix's dueling with my own and Lucan's now curling around my earlobe.

They finally earned one of those moans, reverberating through my chest alongside the rush of pleasure. I clutched at Lucan's collar, Darius's shirt, rocking instinctively, propelled by so much need I couldn't hold myself back.

"We've got you, Lady Noble," Darius said in a voice that nearly melted me. He shoved up my skirt and gripped my panties. "I fucking love these dresses. And they make it so much easier to get right where I want to go."

Then he tore the panties from my hips with one swift jerk. I was already yanking at his fly. As his rigid cock sprang free, Felix passed over a packet with a crinkle of foil.

I laughed. "Of course you'd be prepared."

He nuzzled the side of my head and nipped my ear. "They're all for you going forward, Firebird. But I don't mind sharing with my brothers."

He grazed his teeth along the corner of my jaw as Lucan tugged my mouth to meet his. Then Darius was thrusting into me, and I was lost completely in the heady rush of sensation.

He filled me so completely that a gasp burst from my lips at the jolt of pleasure. Lucan drank in that sound and devoured me further, Felix stroked my uncovered breast, and Darius plunged in and out of me with rasps of breath that sounded almost desperate.

"Our lady," he muttered. "You won't be anyone else's. Not as long as I'm around to have a say in it."

I hummed eagerly and let out another moan. "Fine by me," I said between pants. "Don't want anyone else. Never did. Can't imagine I ever will."

He pounded deeper and deeper, stretching me in just the right ways. The delicious heat of that friction spread all through my torso. I bucked to meet him, kissing Lucan back and then turning to Felix again, my fingers twisted into shirts on either side.

My head felt as if it were soaring right off my body on a surge of bliss. And then I cracked right open under a wave of ecstasy that had me shaking as I clenched around Darius.

He groaned and spilled himself a moment later, ramming himself as deep as he could go one final time. Then, while I was still quaking with the aftermath, he lifted me off the boxes and spun me around.

Some silent communication must have passed between the brothers. The next thing I knew, I was bracing my elbows against the nearest box, leaning forward as Felix hopped down to the ground beside me.

He stroked his hand over my bared ass, and there was the crinkle of another packet. His finger traced over my other opening.

"We'll save this for another time when we've got all the proper supplies to make it fantastic for you," he said, his voice dripping with promise. "For now..." He curled his other hand against my pussy and inhaled sharply at the slickness of my arousal. "I can't believe it's been this long. Seven fucking years. I'm never waiting more than a day again."

Another giggle fell from my lips, followed by a hitch of needy breath as he surged into me from behind. I might have just come, and hard, but it only took a few thrusts of Felix's shaft before the trembling was spreading through my limbs all over again.

But I had one other brother to keep in mind. I tugged Lucan's arm, directing him to perch on the edge of the box near where I'd been sitting before.

"I want another taste of you," I murmured.

"Hell, yes." He scooted closer and freed his cock from his slacks. I let the swaying brought by Felix's strokes propel me over his brother's straining erection.

As I took it into my mouth, Felix let out a low whistle. "That's our girl," he said, his voice bright with awe even as his breaths turned ragged.

"Our *lady*," Darius insisted, not done with me yet. He knelt down at my other side and lapped my nipple into his mouth to test his teeth on it.

I gasped at the sparks that shot through my nerves and sucked harder on Lucan's cock. Heat swelled all through my core with Felix's rhythm inside me. He dipped over my back, kissing my spine and tucking his hand between us. His fingers circled my clit.

"Fuck!" I cried at the quivers that simple touch set off. I closed my lips around Lucan again, determined to bring him with me when I came. I was hurtling toward that edge already, careening along at a heady pace with each thrust and suck.

I bucked back into Felix and worked over Lucan with all the tricks of tongue and teeth I'd learned. Felix pinched my clit just as Darius lapped my breast, and my mouth tightened around Lucan's cock.

With the first salty spurt of his cum in the back of my throat, I unraveled, my pussy clamping so tight around Felix's shaft that he hissed as he came too. We swayed to a stop together, Lucan caressing his fingers over my hair as I swallowed, all of our chests heaving from the glorious exertion.

"Worth the wait," Felix said with a chuckle, and hugged me from behind before withdrawing.

Darius eased me down onto his lap. I settled there, bonelessly sated, and reached for my other two men. But as they sank next to us on either side, Lucan slipping his hand over my thigh and Felix tipping his head against my shoulder, a worry started to nibble at the blissful peace that'd briefly settled over me.

"I don't know if it's going to be enough," I said, and motioned to the bodies slumped beyond the storage area. "If *they're* going to be enough—for Ezra. He didn't believe it was possible that Holly could have masterminded some complicated scheme, and he's not here to see the evidence directly."

"Sexist bastard," Felix remarked.

"He isn't alone in that." I paused. "And Holly and Brant weren't *really* alone in brewing their war. If I had an idea that could give me a more prominent fall guy and solve your biggest problem too…"

I didn't need to finish my sentence. Darius tightened his embrace and kissed the spot just behind my ear. "Whatever you need, Lady Noble. We're here with you all the way."

TWENTY-FOUR

Anthea

IT WAS HOLLY, really, who gave me the idea. So I'd thank her wretched soul for that, wherever it was now hanging out in Hell.

We got back to the Rosano brownstone a little after ten, arriving in our separate cars. At that hour, there was still some activity around the house, but it had a quieter quality—a hushed conversation in a corner of a room here, a hasty snack run into the kitchen there. There were maybe half a dozen lackeys still up and either watching over the house or sorting out other work on the first floor.

The second floor was even quieter. Lucan checked and confirmed that Marcel had headed up to his own third-floor retreat opposite the brothers' apartment. Then Darius let us into the old man's office.

We stood in the darkened space where Holly had once claimed she'd found me snooping, and he turned toward me.

"You don't need to be here for this. We can handle it ourselves."

I shook my head. "It's my plan. It's to settle things between me and Ezra too." I'd have a lot harder time getting out from under my brother's thumb if I couldn't hand him a solid victory. My lips formed a crooked smile. "Anyway, you might need me. Look at how handy I've already been."

"In more ways than one," Felix teased, leaning in to kiss the side of my neck and making my pulse jump.

Darius shot him a baleful look. "Think with your head instead of your dick for five minutes, Don Juan. We've got to play this right, or we'll have a ton more problems instead of none."

I glanced around the room. "What's in here that your dad would really hate having messed with? What's the private stuff everyone should know not to touch?"

Lucan followed my gaze with the sharper analytical precision of familiarity. He pointed to a glossy black cabinet near the desk that had glass doors on the upper half and three drawers with locks lower down. "Those drawers. Only Dad and Darius have the key. Dad's got financial documents in there—deeds and licenses —notes about the business operations. I don't even know what else. But he always made it clear to us that it was a big deal if he showed us something out of there."

"*I* don't even know what all he's got stashed away," Darius said. He fished his keyring out of his pocket and slid a small, simple key off the ring. "But we don't need to. We only need to know there's no way that prick should be going in there. I'll tell Dad that I noticed the key missing after I took a shower and came right to see what was up."

"You should get your hair wet, then," I pointed out. "You wouldn't have stopped to blow-dry it. Gotta sell the story all the way."

Felix chuckled and held his hand out for the key. "Go take care of that, big bro. We can get everything else set up."

Darius grumbled a bit but ducked out of the office to hurry to the nearby bathroom.

Felix walked over to the cabinet and fit the key into the lock of the upper drawer. He looked over his shoulder at me. "Should I open it?"

I considered the staging. "It'd be better if we can get *him* to open it up, so he'll be in just the right position. If he comes in and notices it's open right off the bat, it might put him more on guard, don't you think?"

Lucan nodded. "He's going to think it's odd as soon as he gets here and it's just us, not Marcel, though."

"You want to keep him in an urgent emotional state," I said. "Act like there's a big rush, like his job could depend on him following through ASAP. When people are worried, they don't think about the details as much."

"Of course. We can manage that." He considered me. "He'll also think it's strange that you're here with us."

"I can add to the story," I said, and sat down in a chair near the window. "Felix, you can be guarding me. Make it look like whatever's going on, it's something big to do with the Nobles—that Marcel is finally going to use the leverage he thinks he's got in me. That'll have Griffin even more eager."

As Felix walked over to join me, pulling out his gun, Darius barreled back into the room. He'd done a good job, dampening his hair and then giving it a hasty rub with a towel so it didn't look like he'd just splashed himself or something. When he caught my eye, I gave him a thumbs up.

Lucan lifted his phone. "Are we ready? I can text him over here now."

Darius took out his own pistol, holding it close by his hip. I motioned for him to stay close to the door. "You'll need the angle to look like you burst in and caught him in the act. Make sure you stay between him and the door."

"Got it." He motioned to Lucan. "Bring him in."

Lucan tapped out a text and then took a post next to the desk, standing tensed as if braced for action. Darius stayed to the side of the door, keeping the gun out of view. Felix teased the muzzle of his gun in a slow, delicate circle along the back of my neck.

"Don't worry," he said when I shivered. "The safety's on."

I let out a light chuckle. "That wasn't a *bad* shiver."

"Hmm. Now I'm having all sorts of fun ideas."

"Save them for later," Darius muttered.

Felix shot him a narrow look. "I think by now I've proven that I can carry my own weight in this family just fine."

Darius blinked, momentarily chagrinned. "You're right," he said, still gruffly but with an obvious apology in his tone. "We're a good team—all three of us together."

"All *four*," I piped up.

"Don't worry, Firebird," Felix said, giving my neck

another stroke with the gun. "No one's forgetting you any time soon."

Darius drew himself up straighter. "Footsteps," he said under his breath. "Probably Griffin."

We all fell silent, settling into our roles. Just as the footsteps came close enough that I could hear them from across the room, Lucan thumped his hand against the desk. "We've got to get moving on this," he said in an almost frantic tone. "If we don't get everything ready in time…"

He was setting the stage. Good.

Griffin pushed the door aside and marched into the room. He took in the scene with his beady eyes, stalling just a couple of steps from the door.

"What's going on?" he demanded. "I thought you said Marcel needed me."

"He does," Darius said, quickly and firmly. "He'll be back in a moment—there were too many things he needed to take care of. We've got to strike fast if we're going to get the better of the Nobles. Grab the notebook from that drawer, and we can get started." He jerked his hand toward the cabinet.

To give the appearance that he was too busy to take care of the task himself, Lucan had thrown himself into pawing through the papers and books Marcel had left on his desk. Griffin hustled across the room, knelt by the drawer, and then paused, glancing around at us again. He knit his forehead, a frown crossing his face.

"What exactly are we doing?"

"We got something important out of her," Felix jumped in, waving his gun toward me. "Get a move on, man, or Dad'll be pissed. Any second now, we'll have Nobles crashing in on us."

He was a good enough actor to convey a genuine-sounding panic. It spurred Griffin to action just enough to get his hand to close on the key and twist it in the lock. But as he jerked the drawer open and Darius's gun hand whipped upward, Griffin's head snapped around to stare at me again.

"You're setting me up. Just your brother's puppet, huh? And you convinced them too."

Darius hesitated, still aiming at Griffin but not firing yet. He glanced at me, and my pulse hiccupped with the fear that I'd see suspicion in his gaze. But instead he only raised his eyebrows in a hint of a question, his expression nothing but determined.

He trusted me. He was simply asking if I thought he should go ahead and shoot or find out what this prick had to say.

I blinked at Griffin, not entirely sure myself. "What are you talking about? None of this was Ezra's idea. He'd be pissed if he knew what they're doing."

I made my voice as frantic as possible, but Griffin had spotted Darius's gun, of course. He knew the situation wasn't what we'd said at first.

His hand crept toward the bulge of his own pistol at the back of his jeans, and Darius gave his gun a little shake. "Hands in front, or I'll shoot you without hearing what you're blathering about. I don't care either way."

Griffin froze, his jaw working. He turned his attention on me again. "Do you really think a gang boss would let his kid sister go running around loose making her own plans?" he sneered at me. "He had to know we'd strike back at him. He wanted you in here getting sympathy for your side so you'd take out everyone who's against him. I'll bet he made it sound like family loyalty, as if that means anything. He just wanted to use you."

His words sank into me with a jab of horror. That was what my dad had done for all those years, wasn't it? Forced me into compliance for the good of the family business, used me for his own ends without caring what I thought.

The disdain in Ezra's voice when he'd dismissed my claims about Holly echoed up from my memory, and my stomach twisted. Had he really expected me to come here and use my own judgment, or had he simply figured I'd wreak enough havoc to make his own job easier, one way or another? Maybe he'd even been clever enough to realize that scoffing at me would spur me to further action.

There was a moment, just a second or two, when I wavered. I was so fucking done with being anyone's dupe. But Felix set a gentle hand on my shoulder, Lucan caught my eye from across the room, and Darius adjusted his grip on his gun, his aim never shifting.

Griffin had gambled wrong. He didn't understand that I wasn't here only because of my family or even mostly on Ezra's behalf, not anymore. And what we were doing here was for the men I'd fallen for at least as much as it would help my brother. If my ends happened to eliminate an enemy of the Nobles, it was a happy coincidence, not a mistake.

I was calling the shots here, and not one man in this room or outside it was going to control me ever again.

I gave Darius just the slightest tip of my head, and he pulled the trigger.

The blast propelled Griffin's body against the cabinet, his ruined head smacking the drawers. It left an imprint of blood and bits of skull on the shiny wood as his body sagged lifelessly to the floor.

A shout from below told us the lackeys were already coming running at the noise. Darius made a sweeping gesture for the rest of us to clear out. The story was supposed to be that he'd discovered Griffin on his own, after all.

Felix and I dashed to join Lucan, shoving past the door and ducking into the nearby lounge room before the incoming underlings had made it to the top of the stairs. Lucan planted himself in front of the door and exhaled in a rush.

"It's done," Felix said in an awed whisper. "The creep is dead. No more challengers for the throne. Not that I was ever much of a contender anyway."

Lucan caught his gaze. "Darius was right. We're in this together from here out." His attention slid to me. "Will this be enough to satisfy your brother? You don't think he did have bigger plans?"

I inclined my head, a belated sense of relief washing over me. It *was* done, my whole mission here, in a way that was still sinking in.

I'd gone into the lion's den and emerged not only intact but with three new allies on my side—allies and friends and lovers, who stood with *me*, not with Ezra.

"I'll tell him I found out a major lieutenant of Marcel's was in on the scheme," I said. "You'll need to make him right with his end of the deal and offer some kind of amends for the takeover downtown, but I think you can rebuild the good will there now that the source of the problem is dealt with. Maybe Ezra knew more than he let on… but I don't think it matters. I would have done the same thing no matter how it benefitted him."

Felix slipped his hand around my arm. "You finished the mission you came here on. Does that mean you'll be going back under his roof?"

"No," I said without hesitation. The certainty had been gathering inside me for a while now, potent enough that I felt comfortable voicing it out loud. "I think it's time I stood on my own two feet." I shot him a coy sideways look. "Although I won't mind if certain men lift me off those feet from time to time."

He grinned back at me. "I'm sure we'll all be more than happy to oblige."

Lucan had started tapping on his phone again. "We'd better get the goods moved out of the building where Holly and Brant had them stashed—as much as we can while still leaving a bit to sell the story you presented. I'll see if I can track down any of the money they stole too. We'll square things away with the Nobles."

His gaze flicked upward with a sly glint. "And we wouldn't want there to be any chance of the cops finding the wrong DNA evidence at the scene after what those boxes have been through."

I snorted, and Felix let out a muffled guffaw. I stepped forward, tugging him with me. "All right. Let's go pick up the pieces of this mess and fit them into a better picture."

TWENTY-FIVE

One month later

Anthea

THE BEST THING about the apartment was the windows. A whole wall of them stretched from the living room through the master bedroom, floor to ceiling, giving a view over the south end of Manhattan and the East River beyond. It wasn't quite the penthouse level of the new modern building, but I figured there was nothing wrong with leaving something to aspire to.

The morning sunlight spilled through the glass over my skin. I inhaled deeply, drinking in the warmth in every possible way.

"It's perfect," I said. "I'm taking it."

Darius walked over and wrapped his arms around me

from behind. "Finally we found an abode that our Lady Noble is satisfied with."

I swatted his bicep. "Hey, I had a lot of important criteria. Some of which should be important to *you* too." Like my vicinity to Brooklyn, so the Rosano brothers could drop by on a regular basis. And the very wide master bedroom, which was going to allow for a custom bed large enough for four, if I had anything to say about it.

Felix sauntered up beside us and elbowed his older brother mischievously. "Don't give her a hard time, or maybe she'll decide this one isn't good enough after all."

Lucan had gone to stand by the windows, gazing out over the city. "We'll need to get you a good security system."

Always the most practical one. I shot him an affectionate smile. "I trust you to recommend the best options for me to pick from."

My phone rang in my purse. I fished it out of my purse and stepped away from Darius when I saw the caller ID. "It's my brother."

The three men remained still and silent as I answered the call. "Hi, Ezra."

"Anthea," he said, careful but not cutting. He'd been less stern with me since I'd announced my intentions to move to New York permanently. "I thought I'd check in and see where you're at—and whether there's anything to report as far as the Hell Kickers are concerned."

As far as Ezra knew, part of my new role in the criminal underworld we all moved in was as liaison between him and the Rosanos—with me being more on his side than theirs. It was part of the way I'd sold him on not fighting with me about this additional bid for independence.

Over the past few weeks, with his business in Brooklyn restored to him and the true culprits of the deal-gone-wrong revealed, my brother had re-established a tentative peace with Marcel. But neither the guys nor I were telling our respective families that we were involved in a lot more than business when it came to each other.

Our personal lives were none of their concern. And frankly, my family had already gotten to dictate too much of what happened in mine. The three men around me and I had made our commitments to each other, and that was all that mattered, not anyone else's opinions.

"I've just found an apartment," I told Ezra. "So I can finally get out of the hotel. Everything seems to be going smoothly here with the recent joint operations between the Hell Kickers and your local business. You know I'd contact you as soon as I saw any reason to worry."

"Of course." He sighed. "Are you sure you won't reconsider? I'd feel better having you close at hand—for your own security. You've been through enough already."

He didn't know the half of it. But he also didn't know how much joy I'd found here that I couldn't imagine getting anywhere near back in Paradise Bend.

Besides, I was pretty sure what he was *really* most concerned about was keeping a tight leash on me and my skills, which I'd just proven were even more valuable than he'd expected.

"I think it's time I spread my wings a little," I said lightly. "We've talked about this. It'll be good for me to establish connections of my own and broaden the Nobles reach that way. If you ever need me for a job, all you've got to do is give me a call."

My success at uncovering the rot inside the Hell Kickers had also made it impossible for him to argue that I couldn't hold my own. He hummed noncommittally but couldn't actually offer up any solid reasons why I should come back into the fold. He was smart enough to realize that as long as I wasn't outright defying him on any essential matter, having a happy ally was more important than having that ally nearby.

"If anything goes sideways, don't hesitate to reach out to me," he said.

"I know you've got my back." I just couldn't be totally sure he wouldn't be standing there fitting a collar around my neck if I gave him the chance. "I'll stop by just to visit regularly too."

I wanted to keep an eye on Wylder, make sure Ezra wasn't pushing my nephew too hard now that he'd lost his grip on both his older son and me. The kid needed to have someone around who'd have *his* back without any alternate agenda.

Just seconds after I'd hung up, my second phone—the one I'd set up for my new line of work—pinged with an incoming text. I swapped it for my regular phone, glancing at the message.

I hear you deal in accidents and illnesses. I may have a job for you.

Another smile tugged at my lips. With the help of the Rosano brothers, I'd been surreptitiously getting word out on the streets that for anyone who needed help of the subtle variety, either committing a crime they didn't want to look like a crime or investigating a supposed accident that they thought might *not* be one, I was the new resident expert. I'd already handled a couple of jobs that'd covered my hotel stay and the deposit I'd need for this apartment.

"Looks like I've got another client," I told the men, waggling the phone. "Business is picking up!"

"Soon you'll be queen of New York City," Felix teased, moving in to nuzzle my neck. "I love watching you get down to work." He paused, his body going still next to mine, and pulled back just far enough to meet my eyes. His gaze seemed to search mine for a moment before he said, "I love *you*."

My breath caught in my throat. Then Darius was giving his brother a light cuff to the shoulder, scowling at him. "Leaping in ahead of everyone like always. Can't you *ever* cut us a break?"

"Obviously we shouldn't have expected anything else," Lucan said with a bemused shake of his head.

I looked around at the three of them. "What are you talking about?"

"We were *going* to say it all together," Darius growled, shooting another half-hearted glower at Felix before turning to me. His expression softened. "Pick out a necklace or a bracelet or something as a symbol…"

"A ring seems too obvious when you want to keep things quiet," Lucan put in.

Tears pricked at the back of my eyes with the wave of emotion that swept through me, but there was nothing but joy in them. "I don't need a symbol," I said. "What matters is that I have *you*. I love you too, all of you."

"Good," Darius grumbled playfully, tugging me away

from Felix into his own arms. "Because it's been enough trouble falling for you. If you didn't feel the same way, I'd just give up on saying it to anyone."

I nudged him with my elbow. "You haven't actually said it yet."

He huffed and bowed his head next to mine. His breath tickled over my ear when he spoke. "I love you, Lady Noble. You're it for me, in case that wasn't obvious."

Lucan grasped my hand. "And for me. I loved you when I was seventeen, and I only love you more now that I've seen the woman you've become."

As Felix eased in to enclose me completely in a circle of heat, my phone chimed with another text. The youngest Rosano brother nipped my earlobe. "Put the asshole clients off for an hour or two. You don't want to look too available. And I believe *we* need to christen your new digs."

I snorted, but I couldn't stop myself from beaming at the same time. "I haven't even signed the lease yet."

"But you will," Darius said. "I think Felix has exactly the right idea."

As he sought out my lips and Lucan slipped his arm around my waist, I decided it *was* a pretty good idea. A moment like this deserved a celebration with the men I'd fallen for, the men I was staying for.

Possibly for the first time in my life, the ground beneath my feet felt perfectly solid. And as long as I had them standing with me, that ground stretched out toward all kinds of horizons I couldn't wait to claim as my own.

ABOUT THE AUTHOR

Eva Chance is a pen name for contemporary romance written by Amazon top 100 bestselling author Eva Chase. If you love gritty romance, dominant men, and fierce women who never have to choose, look no further.

Eva lives in Canada with her family. She loves stories both swoony and supernatural, and strong women and the men who appreciate them.

Connect with Eva online:
www.evachase.com
eva@evachase.com

9 781990 338984